About *The Corpse Washer*

Young Jawad, born to a tradition[al] Shi'ite family of corpse washers and shrouders in Baghdad, decides to abandon the family tradition, choosing instead to become a sculptor, to celebrate life rather than tend to death. He enters Baghdad's Academy of Fine Arts in the late 1980s, in defiance of his father's wishes and determined to forge his own path. But the circumstances of history dictate otherwise. Saddam Hussein's dictatorship and the economic sanctions of the 1990s destroy the socioeconomic fabric of society. The 2003 invasion and military occupation unleash sectarian violence. Corpses pile up, and Jawad returns to the inevitable washing and shrouding. Trained as an artist to shape materials to represent life aesthetically, he now must contemplate how death shapes daily life and the bodies of Baghdad's inhabitants.

Through the struggles of a single desperate family, Sinan Antoon's novel shows us the heart of Iraq's complex and violent recent history. Descending into the underworld where the borders between life and death are blurred and where there is no refuge from unending nightmares, Antoon limns a world of great sorrows, a world where the winds wail.

The Corpse Washer

The Corpse Washer

SINAN ANTOON

TRANSLATED FROM THE ARABIC BY THE AUTHOR

YALE UNIVERSITY PRESS ■ NEW HAVEN & LONDON

A MARGELLOS
WORLD REPUBLIC OF LETTERS BOOK

The Margellos World Republic of Letters is dedicated to making literary works from around the globe available in English through translation. It brings to the English-speaking world the work of leading poets, novelists, essayists, philosophers, and playwrights from Europe, Latin America, Africa, Asia, and the Middle East to stimulate international discourse and creative exchange.

Yale University Press books may be purchased in quantity for educational, business, or promotional use. For information, please e-mail sales.press@yale.edu (U.S. office) or sales@yaleup.co.uk (U.K. office).

Set in Electra type by Keystone Typesetting, Inc. Printed in the United States of America.

The Library of Congress has cataloged the hardcover edition as follows:
Anṭūn [Antoon], Sinān, 1967–. [Wahdaha shajarat al-rumman. English]
The corpse washer / Sinan Antoon; translated from the Arabic by the author.
    pages   cm.—(A Margellos world republic of letters book.)
"First published in 2010 in Arabic as Wahdaha shajarat al-rumman by al-Mu'assasah al-'Arabiyah lil-Dirasat wa-al-Nashr, Beirut, Lebanon"—Title page verso.
ISBN 978-0-300-19060-1 (cloth : alk. paper)
I. Title.
PJ7914.N88W3413 2013
892.7'37—dc23
2013002091

ISBN 978-0-300-20564-0 (pbk.)

A catalogue record for this book is available from the British Library.

CONTENTS

PREFACE

"A poem is never finished, only abandoned," according to Paul Valéry. This is often true. Can one say the same about a novel?

Novels do end, of course, with the last word on the last page. But even before becoming a writer I always wondered as a young reader about the lives and trajectories of events after the act of reading comes to an end. As a novelist I still wonder what became of my characters. Alas, there is no way to communicate with them. I know more about the characters and the events than I have written on paper, but I don't know everything.

Novels inhabit a liminal space between the real and the imaginary. The experience of translating my own novel has allowed me to return to that space and to inhabit it once again, temporarily. This time, however, the characters spoke English. Their lives (and deaths) did not change at all, but they said a few words here and there differently and left a few others unsaid.

All this is to say that when the translator inhabits the body and being of the author, s/he is given unique privileges that are otherwise denied or frowned upon.

New York, August 2012

The Corpse Washer

In both gardens are fruit, palm trees, and pomegranates

The Qur'an

ONE

She is lying naked on her back on a marble bench in an open place with no walls or ceilings. There is no one around and nothing in sight except the sand. I, too, am naked, barefoot, dumbfounded by everything around me. I can feel the sand under my feet and a cool wind. I move slowly toward the bench. When and why has she come back after all these years? Her long black hair is piled about her head. A few locks cover her right cheek, as if guarding her face, which has not changed with the years. Her eyebrows are carefully plucked, and her eyelids, which end in thick eyelashes, are shut. Her nose guards her lips, which bear pink lipstick as if she were still alive. Her nipples are erect; there is no trace of the surgery. Her hands are clasped over her navel; her fingernails and toenails are painted the same pink as her lipstick. Her pubic hair is shaved.

I wonder whether she is asleep or dead. I am afraid to touch her. I look into her face and whisper her name, "Reem." She smiles, her eyes still shut at first. Then she opens them, and the blackness in her pupils smiles as well. I can't grasp what is going on. I ask in a loud voice, "Reem, what are you doing here?"

I am about to hug and kiss her, but she warns me: "Don't kiss me. Wash me first so we can be together and then . . . "

"What? You are still alive?"

"Wash me so we can be together. I missed you so much."

"But you are not dead!"

"Wash me, darling . . . Wash me so we can be together."

"With what? There is nothing here."

"Wash me, darling."

Raindrops begin to fall, and she closes her eyes. I wipe a drop off her nose with my index finger. Her skin is warm, which means she is alive. I start to caress her hair. I will wash her with the rain, I think. She smiles as if she'd heard my thought. Another drop settles above her left eyebrow. I wipe it off.

I think I hear a car approaching. I turn around and see a Humvee driving at an insane speed, leaving a trail of flying dust. It suddenly swerves to the right and comes to a stop a few meters away from us. Its doors open. Masked men wearing khaki uniforms and carrying machine guns rush toward us. I try to shield Reem with my right hand, but one of the men has already reached me. He hits me in the face with the stock of his machine gun. I fall to the ground. He kicks me in the stomach. Another starts dragging me away from the washing bench. None of them says a word. I am screaming and cursing them, but I can't hear myself. Two men force me to get down on my knees and tie my wrists with a wire behind my back. One of them puts a knife to my neck; the other blindfolds me. I try to run away, but they hold me tightly. I scream again, but cannot hear my screams. I hear only Reem's shrieks, the laughter and grunts of the men, the sound of the rain.

I feel a sharp pain, then the cold blade of the knife penetrating my neck. Hot blood spills over my chest and back. My head falls to the ground and rolls like a ball on the sand. I hear footsteps. One of the men takes off my blindfold and shoves it into his pocket. He spits in my face and goes away. I see my body to the left of the bench, kneeling in a puddle of blood.

The other men return to the Humvee, two of them dragging Reem by her arms. She tries to turn her head back in my direction, but one of them slaps her. I cry out her name but can't hear my voice. They put her in the back seat and shut the door. The engine starts. The Humvee speeds away and disappears over the horizon. The rain keeps falling on the empty bench.

I woke up panting and sweating. I wiped my forehead and face. The same nightmare had been recurring for weeks, with minor changes.

Sometimes I saw Reem's severed head on the bench and heard her voice saying, "Wash me, darling," but this was the first time there was rain. It must have slipped into my dream from outdoors. I could hear drops on the window next to my bed.

I looked at my watch. It was already 3:30 A.M.

I've slept only three hours after a long and grueling day. I am worn out.

Death is not content with what it takes from me in my waking hours, it insists on haunting me even in my sleep. Isn't it enough that I toil all day tending to its eternal guests, preparing them to sleep in its lap? Is death punishing me because I thought I could escape its clutches? If my father were still alive he would mock my silly thoughts. He would dismiss all this as infantile, unbecoming to a man. Didn't he spend a lifetime doing his job day after day, never once complaining of death? But death back then was timid and more measured than today.

I can almost hear death saying: "I am what I am and haven't changed at all. I am but a postman."

If death is a postman, then I receive his letters every day. I am the one who opens carefully the bloodied and torn envelopes. I am the one who washes them, who removes the stamps of death and dries and perfumes them, mumbling what I don't entirely believe in. Then I wrap them carefully in white so they may reach their final reader—the grave.

But letters are piling up, Father! Tenfold more than what you used to see in the span of a week now pass before me in a day or two. If you were alive, Father, would you say that that is fate and God's will? I wish you were here so I could leave Mother with you and escape without feeling guilty. You were heavily armed with faith, and that made your heart a castle. My heart, by contrast, is an abandoned house whose windows are shattered and doors unhinged. Ghosts play inside it, and the winds wail.

As a child, I would cover my head with a second pillow to block out noise. I look for it now; it has fallen by the bed next to my slippers. I pick it up and bury my head under it in order to reclaim my share of the night. The image of Reem being dragged away by her hair keeps returning.

Reem hadn't been at the heart of my nightmare until a few weeks ago. Where was she now? I heard a few years ago that she was in Amsterdam. I'll Google her again tomorrow when I go to the Internet café after work. I'll try a different spelling of her name in English and maybe I'll find something. But can I just grab a bit of sleep for an hour or two?

TWO

I stood next to my mother on the steps in front of the big wooden door. Her right hand firmly clasped my right hand, as if I were about to run or fly away. Her left hand carried the *sufurtas* in which she packed my father's lunch—three small copper pots, each stacked on top of the other in a metal skeleton resembling a little metal building. The top pot was filled with rice. The middle one with okra stew and two pieces of meat. The lower pot usually had some fruit. That day she'd put in a tiny bunch of white grapes, the kind we call "goat nipples," that my father liked. There was a warm loaf of homemade bread in the nylon sack dangling from her left wrist. She put her left foot on the steps and temporarily released my hand to knock four times. Her strong knocks pushed the door open. She pretended not to see the young man squatting a few steps away from the door with his back to the wall. He was wearing black. His head was buried in his hands and he looked like he was wailing. Smoke rose from the cigarette in his left hand. That was the first time I'd seen a grown man cry.

I looked into my mother's coffee-colored eyes. In a hushed voice, I asked, "Why is this man crying?"

She put her index finger on her lips to shush me and whispered, "Don't be rude, Jawad!"

I craned to the left, curious to see what was happening inside. It was the first time my mother had taken me to my father's place of work. He usually took the *sufurtas* with him in the morning, but that day he had forgotten to bring it along.

The narrow walkway led to a wide room with a high ceiling.

Three or four men were standing at its entrance with their backs blocking the scene. Were they watching my father as he worked? The street was quiet and although the walkway was long, I could hear the sound of water being spilled, with my father's voice muttering phrases I couldn't understand, except for the word "God."

My mother knocked at the open door with more force and determination this time and then called out "Hammoudy." None of the men turned around. Then the one standing to the far left moved aside and Hammoudy's face appeared. He limped to the door. Hammoudy, my father's assistant, looked older than his actual age. He had black hair and eyelashes as thick as a paint brush. He wore blue shorts and a white T-shirt which was wet in many spots. After exchanging a quick hello, my mother gave him the *sufurtas* and the bread saying: "Here, Hammoudy, this is Abu Ammoury's lunch. He forgot to take it."

He thanked her and rushed back inside after shutting the door. She held my hand again and we started to make our way back home. I turned back to look at the squatting man. His head was still in his hands. My mother shook me and said, "Mind where you're going. You're going to trip and fall."

At that age I didn't know much about my father's work. All I knew was that he was a *mghassilchi*, a body-washer, but this word was obscure to me. I was afraid that day and asked my mother: "Does Father hurt people?"

"No son, not at all. It's quite the opposite. Why do you ask?"

"But wasn't that man there crying?"

"Yes, but not because of your father. He's just sad."

"Why is he sad? What are they doing inside?"

"Your dad washes the bodies of the dead. It's a very honorable profession and those who do it are rewarded by God."

"Why does he wash them? Are they dirty?"

"No, but they must be purified."

"And where do the dead go after they die?"

"To God. Your father tends to them before they are buried."

"How can they go to God if they are buried?"

"The soul rises to the sky, but the body remains in the earth it came from. It is said that we are come from Adam and Adam is of dust."

I looked up to the sky. There were five clouds huddled together and I wondered: *Which one will carry the dead man's soul? Where will it take it?*

THREE

The only time I ever saw my father cry was many years later when he heard that my brother Ameer, whom we called Ammoury, had died. Ameer, who was five years my senior, was transformed from "Doctor" into "Martyr." His framed black-and-white photograph occupied the heart of the main wall in our living room and even a bigger part of my father's heart, which Ammoury had already monopolized. Ameer, you see, was the ideal son who had always made my father proud. He always excelled and was the top of his class. At the national baccalaureate exams, his score was 95 percent, which enabled him to go to medical school to study to become a surgeon. Ameer wanted to fulfill his dream of opening a clinic so he could allow Father to retire. Father insisted that he would keep working until he died. Ameer insisted on helping Father at work even on his short leaves from the army during the years of war with Iran. This was before he was killed in the al-Faw battles.

I was reading in my room on the second floor when I heard a car stop in front of the house and doors being slammed shut. Seconds later, I heard the new doorbell ringing—the doorbell Ameer had bought and installed after the old one had stopped working and I had procrastinated about fixing it. I drew the curtain open and saw a taxi with a flag-draped coffin on top of it. My heart sunk into an abyss.

Whenever I saw a taxi driving down the street with a flag-draped coffin on it, the thought would cross my mind that Ammoury might one day return like this, but I would quickly cast the vision aside. I rushed down the stairs barefoot. When I reached the front door my mother was already out in the street in her nightgown without her *abaya*. She stood next to the taxi, beating her head, staring at the coffin and screaming "Oh my . . . Ammoury . . . Ammoury . . . Ammoury's gone . . . My son is gone."

A uniformed man stood there observing the scene. He asked me to sign the papers confirming receipt of the body. Without so much as a glance at the papers, I signed two copies with the ballpoint pen he gave me. I handed back the papers and the pen. He returned the pen to his pocket and said, "May God have mercy on him. My condolences." He gave me a sheet of paper which I folded and put in my shirt pocket.

The neighbors had come out of their houses after hearing my mother's wailing. Some of them stood around the taxi and a number of women rushed to console my mother and join in her wailing. The bald taxi driver had untied the ropes which secured the coffin on top of the metal rack. He put them in his trunk and stood waiting. I went up to my mother to hug her, but she was hysterical and surrounded by women who had started beating their heads as well. I wondered how my father's weak heart would take the news.

The driver started moving the coffin around, as if to hint that we were to help him. I heard a voice saying "Go to Abu Ammoury's place and inform him." I yelled out that I would tell him myself after we brought down the coffin. The driver and I and some of the young neighborhood men lifted the coffin and brought it inside the house, placing it in the living room.

A silent tear fell on my cheek as I rushed to deliver the news of Ammoury's death to my father. Ammoury, who used to play soccer with me on the street. Ammoury, who one summer had taught me how to make a paper kite using twigs from palm trees and who had climbed the neighbor's palm tree to retrieve my kite when it got stuck there. Ammoury, with whom I shared a room for twenty years and who used to snore sometimes. Ammoury, who had caught me masturbating in the bathroom once when I forgot to lock the door and who had apologized, smiled, and quickly closed the door. He told me later that it was a natural desire, but said I shouldn't overdo it. Ammoury, who gave me his blue twenty-four-inch bike when he became taller and bought a twenty-six. Ammoury, who used to race me and would always let me win at the end. Ammoury, who had kept my secret and agreed to go to the high school headmaster instead of my father to persuade him to allow me back to classes after I had been absent too many times. Ammoury, who had genuinely tried to understand my artistic tendencies and my decision to study sculpture and who truly respected art even though it was really not his thing. Ammoury, who had wanted me to be an engineer or a doctor like him and who couldn't hide his disappointment when I scored 87.7 percent on the baccalaureate exams. It was enough to enter the Academy of Fine Arts, but that wasn't his hope for his little brother. Ammoury, who used to stand by me at home, defending my point of view against my parents' criticisms and who would tell them I was talented and had to choose my own path and take responsibility for my decisions. Ammoury, who had visited the exhibition we had during our second year at the academy to encourage me and who had asked me to explain the idea behind my piece and expressed his admiration, listening attentively. Ammoury, who used to joke with me thinking he was encouraging me, but who actually annoyed me, by saying that my statues would one day populate the squares of Baghdad.

Dr. Ammoury, the handsome, shy one but who nonetheless succeeded in charming Wasan, our neighbor, and made her fall in love with him. My mother rushed to ask for her hand so they would be engaged before his graduation. He was drafted into the army after graduation, but died before they got married. Wasan, with her long black hair and lovely legs, a student of architecture at the University of Baghdad. I felt guilty when I couldn't drive her away from my sexual fantasies. Ammoury, of whom I was greatly jealous, because he was the favorite, pampered—an ideal I could never approach. I felt guilty because I couldn't stop myself, even in this moment, from wondering so selfishly: *Would the news of my own death in this seemingly endless war leave a quarter of the pain and sorrow that*

Ammoury's departure will have left behind? I wiped my tears and scolded myself for this utter narcissism.

I got to the *mghaysil,* the washhouse. The door was ajar. I crossed the walkway and saw the Qur'anic verse "Every soul shall taste death" in beautiful Diwani script hanging over the door. The yellowish paint on the wall was peeling away because of the humidity from the washing. Father was sitting in the left corner of the side room on a wooden chair listening to the radio. Death's traces—its scents and memories—were present in every inch of that place. As if death were the real owner and Father merely an employee working for it and not for God, as he liked to think.

Death, ever present in Father's place of work and his days, was about to declare its presence once again, but with a cruelty and force that would tattoo itself on Father's heart and on what was left of his years. The washing bench was empty and dry. Father's yellow amber worry beads were clicking in his right hand. Hammoudy must have gone out to buy something and left him alone. Father's eyes greeted me. He must've heard my footsteps. "Hello, Father."

I had not set foot there for more than a year. I had tried to steer away from death, and my relationship with Father had soured. He must have sensed something in my voice and seen the sadness on my face. There was anxiety in his voice:

"What? Is something wrong with your mother?"

"No, Father."

"What then?"

I approached him and leaned to embrace him as he sat in his chair. He asked me: "What then? Did something happen to Ammoury?"

The news in the past two days had been all about the bloody battles in al-Faw and the heavy casualties inflicted there. Two months earlier, Ammoury's unit had been transferred from the northern sector to al-Faw. I hesitated for a few long seconds trying to postpone the grave news. Then I told him, as I hugged him and kissed his left cheek without being able to stop my tears: "May you have a long life, Father. They just brought him home."

He put his arms around me and repeated in a trembling voice:

"Oh, God. Oh, God. There is no power save in God. There is no power save in God. There is no God but God. Only he is immortal." Then he wept like a child. I hugged him tightly and felt that for a few minutes we'd exchanged the roles of father and son. I sensed he wanted to stand up, so I loosened my arm. He stood up and wiped his tears with the back of his right hand, without letting go of his worry beads. He turned off the radio and put on his jacket. We locked the door and went back home together without exchanging a word.

We didn't wash Ammoury. According to tradition, martyrs are not washed. He was buried in his military uniform. I never saw Father cry after that time, but the grief I saw piercing his eyes and voice that day would resurface every now and then on his face, especially when he gazed at Ammoury's photograph which hung on the wall, as if he were silently conversing with him. It was the same look I saw on Father's face when Ammoury's coffin was being covered with dirt and the gravedigger recited:

> We come from God and to him we return. O God, take his
> soul up to you and show him your approval. Fill his grave with
> mercy so that he may never need any other mercy but yours,
> for he believes in you and your resurrection. This is what God
> and his messenger promised us. Verily they have told the truth.
> O God, grant us more faith and peace.

After the funeral was over the black banner hung for months on the wall at the entrance of our street:

> "Think not of those who die for God as dead,
> but rather alive with their God."
> The martyr Doctor Ameer Kazim Hasan, died in the battles to
> liberate al-Faw on the 17th of April, 1988.

Father had never been very talkative and laughed rarely, but Ammoury's death intensified his silence and dejection and made him more moody and volatile. My mother was the one who had to withstand the waves of his anger with a mumble or a complaint she would whisper to herself when he yelled: "Enough already" or "Turn the

TV down." The TV had become her only solace. I hadn't spent much time at home even before Ammoury's death, but my clashes with Father became more frequent, and I tried to avoid him so as to avoid them. When I came back late at night, he would tell me that I treated our house like a hotel.

In August of 1990, almost three and a half years after Ammoury's death, Saddam invaded Kuwait. To secure the eastern front with Iran and withdraw troops from there to Kuwait, he agreed to all the Iranian conditions and relinquished all the demands for which he'd waged the war in the first place. Father punched the table and shouted: "Why the hell did we fight for eight years then and what in hell did Ammoury die for?"

FOUR

Like all children I was very curious and would pester Father with questions about his work, but he said he'd tell me all about it later when the time was right. I would accompany him when I was old enough. "It's too early, focus on school." Ammoury had started helping Father when he was fifteen and started to wash at eighteen, but my father never allowed me to go inside his workplace. He wanted to keep work and home separate. When I used to ask Ammoury about work, he never gave me satisfying answers; these were matters for grown-ups and I was still a child.

During the summer break after ninth grade Father told me that I could start accompanying him to work to watch and learn the basics of the trade. On the first day, I was ecstatic. I felt a sense of awe as I stood in front of the door. Father moved the *sufurtas* he was carrying from his right hand to his left and put his right hand in his pocket looking for the key. The sky was clear and cloudless that day. I noticed that there was no sign indicating what the place was, and when I asked him he said there was no need for a sign, because it was not a shop or a store. He added, as he turned the key in the lock to open the door, that everyone knew where the *mghaysil* was. It was the only such place for Shiites in Baghdad, and the vast majority of others were off in Najaf. He said that with great pride, adding that everyone in Kazimiyya knew the place.

It was a bit smaller than I had imagined it. The scents of lotus and camphor wafted through the air, and I felt the humidity seeping into my skin. He closed the door behind us and went inside ahead of me. The first object that struck my eyes after we crossed the hallway and entered the main room was the marble bench on which the dead were washed. Its northern part, where their heads would rest, was slightly elevated so that the water could flow down. The *mghaysil* was more than six decades old, and many generations of our family had worked in it, including my grandfather, who had died before I was born. The walls and ceiling were painted a yellowish white, but time and humidity had peeled portions of them, especially on the ceiling. The patches looked like autumn leaves about to fall. My father pressed a button on the wall, and the fan in the middle of the ceiling started to whirl. I looked to the right and saw the coffins brought from the Religious Endowment Center piled in the corner. Close by above them on the wall was a modest window which allowed the sun to illuminate the room. A slant of light had snuck in and left a spot on the floor. The window was above eye level and left the corners a bit dark, but I could see a fragment of the sky. The old ceiling fan traced fluttering wings on the opposite wall. Directly beneath the window was a door leading to a tiny garden where the pomegranate tree my father loved so much stood. Next to the door was a wooden bench on which relatives would wait and watch their beloved dead be washed and shrouded. Six feet away from the marble bench was a big white basin right below a copper-colored water faucet. Copper bowls and jugs were piled inside the basin. My father scorned plastic containers, which had recently become quite common. Under the basin to the left was another faucet with a low wooden stool in front, the kind we used in the bathroom to sit on and wash. To the right of the basin was a big wooden cupboard with glass doors that held the bags and boxes of ground lotus leaves, camphor, shrouds, cotton, and soap.

The marble bench was rectangular and its base was ringed by a moat lined with white ceramic tiles funneling into a small stream that took the water into the tiny garden rather than into the drain— for the water used for washing the dead was never to mix with sewage. From the left-hand corner a small walkway led to the bathroom and a small storage room. On the western wall the Qur'anic verse "Every soul shall taste death" in Diwani script hung within a thick wooden frame right over the wooden door which led to a side room where Father sat most of the time. That room had two wooden chairs separated by a small table. There was only one window, and next to it a portrait of Imam Ali.

Father went in and hung his jacket in the storage room. Then he came back and went to the side room and sat on one of the wooden chairs and turned the radio on, setting the dial to his favorite station. I followed him. He motioned to me to sit down. My eyes wandered again. I don't know why I'd thought that we would start working right away. He said that first I had to just watch him and Hammoudy at the job for a number of weeks. Hammoudy was five years older than I was and had worked with my father from a young age. This was how he began. Afterward I could start to help out and hand him the necessary items. I wouldn't start washing until I'd mastered the preparatory work and had fathomed its meaning. I nodded dutifully. Half an hour later, Hammoudy arrived and asked what he should do. Father asked him to sweep the place and check the cupboards to make sure they were fully stocked. He told me to go with Hammoudy, so I did.

I watched Hammoudy sweep the floor around the marble bench and the corners—although there was really no need to sweep. After he took the broom back to the storage room, he seemed eager to explain the lay of the land to me, proud to display his professional knowledge of the place.

Hammoudy was not the only one in his family who worked as a body washer. His mother, Umm Hammoudy, was also a washer, in charge of the women's *mghaysil*, which lay behind this one and whose door opened onto the next street over. His father had died when he was three. Two years later, his mother married another man, but Hammoudy's stepfather was captured by the Iranians during the war. He was in the popular army militia. Because he never returned after the war ended, he was considered missing in action and presumed dead. No one married her after that. People said that whoever married her would die. Umm Hammoudy had asked my father to take her son on as an assistant, and he agreed. He had left school after tenth grade to help her out and was exempt from military service because of the limp in his right leg which he got when he was hit by a speeding car while riding his bike on one of Kazimiyya's streets.

Hammoudy gave me a quick tour and showed me where the lotus, camphor, cotton, soap, and shrouds were shelved. Then we went to the storage room where the towels and boxes of shrouds and other materials were kept, and where there was also a tiny gas stove to make tea and heat food.

We went to the side room, and Hammoudy brought a third chair from the tiny garden and put it in the room. My father asked him to make some tea. I sat down and skimmed the previous day's newspapers which were lying around. Hammoudy came back with a tray and put it on the table. The scent of cardamom filled the room. My father was intoxicated by the voice of Zuhoor Hussein coming from the radio while our spoons stirred the tea in tiny cups dissolving the sugar. We took sips and put down our cups one by one. Hammoudy took the sports page of *al-Thawra*. A relative calm descended, interrupted half an hour later by loud knocks at the door. Hammoudy darted toward the walkway.

A male voice asked whether this was the *mghaysil*. Hammoudy said that it was and invited him to enter. The voice said that first they would go to the car to get the body. Father turned off the radio and made his way to the door. I put the newspaper down on the table and looked at him, but he seemed unaware of my presence. Five minutes later Hammoudy returned, followed by two men carrying the deceased wrapped in a large white sheet. Hammoudy pointed to the marble bench and they laid him down there.

People used to bring in the dead after obtaining death certificates from the Office of Forensic Medicine. Father was a careful man, so he made sure to read the certificate before washing anyone. The men who brought the body both wore black. The first man was about Father's age, in his early fifties. White had crept into his hair and the sides of his moustache. The pale rims of his brown eyes were red with tears or fatigue. The second man had similar features and hair color, but was younger and stubble-bearded. The older man asked Father about the fee.

"Whatever you can manage," he answered, "plus the cost of the shroud, but later. Who is the deceased?"

"He was our brother," the man said. "He had a stroke."

"There is no power save in God," my father said. "May God have mercy on him and give you long lives."

The elder replied: "May God have mercy on your loved ones."

The younger man didn't say a thing. My father invited them to sit on the bench or to stand if they wished and declared that the washing and shrouding would take about three quarters of an hour. The elder man didn't utter a word and stood next to his brother a few feet away from the washing bench. I stood nearby, leaning on the wall.

Father approached the washing bench from its west side and removed the sheet from the body. The pale face and hollow eyes of a man in his late fifties appeared. I was afraid and felt a tightness in my chest. This was the first time I'd seen a dead man up close. His hair and moustache were grizzled. The moustache was thin, unlike his beard, which looked like it hadn't been shaved for days.

Hammoudy approached the bench from the east side. My father lifted the upper part of the body so that Hammoudy could pull the sheet out from under it. They did the same thing with the lower part and then Hammoudy presented the sheet to the elder brother, who stood still. The dead man had a white undershirt and gray pants on, but was barefoot. His fists were clenched. Father grasped the right fist and opened it gently. Hammoudy did the same with the left fist. They undressed him except for his white underpants. Then Father covered the man's body from his navel to his upper thighs with a white cloth Hammoudy had handed to him. He removed the underpants from under the cloth and handed them to Hammoudy who folded all the clothes and put them in a sack and offered it to the brother.

Father went to the basin and removed his slippers. He took down the white apron, from where it hung on a nail to the left, and put it on. It covered his chest and body down to his knees. He tied the apron strings behind his back and rolled up his sleeves. He took a bar of soap, turned on the faucet and lathered his hands and arms up to his elbows. Then he rinsed them. He repeated this twice more.

While he was drying his hands and arms with a towel, Hammoudy put one of the big bowls under the second faucet. Water was pouring down. He took out two bags from the cupboard. He put one down and opened the second and sprinkled some of what was inside it on top of the water. I began to smell the scent of ground lotus leaves, which I used to detect on Father when he returned home.

Father approached the washing bench from the east side and said in a hushed voice: "In the name of God, most Merciful, most Compassionate. Your forgiveness, O Lord, your forgiveness. Here is the body of your servant who believed in you. You have taken his soul and separated the two. Your forgiveness O Lord, your forgiveness." Then he started to gently wipe the belly to make sure all fluids were out of the body. Hammoudy put a stool close to the bench so that the bowl of water he was about to put on it would be within Father's reach. Then he placed the bowl on the stool and added some ground lotus leaves to it. He put a small metal bowl in the big bowl.

Father filled the small bowl with water and motioned to Hammoudy, who sprinkled some of the ground lotus on the dead man's head. Father started to lather the hair and scrub it. Once the head was washed, Hammoudy helped him turn the man on his side while Father kept repeating: "Your forgiveness. Your forgiveness." He started to wash the right side of the body. First the head, then the right side of the face, neck, shoulder, arm, hand, chest, and belly. He kept pouring water and moving his hand softly along the body, repeating: "Your forgiveness, O Lord, your forgiveness." When he reached the deceased man's hips, he washed his private parts without removing the white cloth. Then he washed the leg, from the thigh to the toes. Then the two of them turned the body onto its back.

Father went to the other side of the bench and they turned the body on its left side to wash it. Father repeated the process with the same meticulousness from the head until he reached the sole of the left foot. Hammoudy had refilled the big bowl and stood waiting to replace the one Father was using. Father went to the basin and cleansed his hands and arms after the first wash. The floor around the bench was wet, but most of the water had gathered in the moat and made its way out into the garden.

Hammoudy took out the camphor bag and crushed two cubes of it, adding the powder to another bowl. Again, Father gently rubbed the deceased's belly and started to wash the right side of the head with the water mixed with camphor and made his way to the toes and then moved to the left side. After finishing the second wash he cleansed his own hands and arms again. The third wash was done with pure water alone.

Father used to lower his eyes as he washed, almost seeming asleep. But his hands washed with strength, without harshness. Afterward he went to the lower faucet and cleansed his hands, arms, and legs up to his knees three times and dried himself with a towel Hammoudy handed him. Then he took another white towel from the cupboard and carefully dried the man's body and gave the towel to Hammoudy, who took it to the storage room.

Father took the camphor bag and measured out a spoonful into a small container. He rubbed some of it on the dead man's forehead, nose, cheeks, chin, palms, knees, and toes—the spots that touch the ground when one prays. Afterward he cleansed his own hands and feet again, as did Hammoudy. Then Father took some cotton and stuffed it into the dead man's nostrils and placed some between the dead man's thighs and turned him over to put some between his buttocks. I later learned this was done so that no blood would leak and pollute the shroud. Then he took a deep breath. Hammoudy brought out a large piece of cloth and a pair of scissors. He handed them to Father, who cut out a big swath. Hammoudy took back the scissors and the remainder of the cloth. My father held the man's thighs tightly and wrapped the piece of cloth around them twice. Hammoudy handed him the rest of the cloth. Father wrapped it around the man's head and tied it under his chin, keeping his face exposed. Then Hammoudy brought out the three parts of the shroud. Father took the first part and spread it over the body, covering the man from the navel to the knees. Then he sprinkled some more camphor on it. Hammoudy handed him the second, bigger piece. Father took it and covered the body from the shoulders to the lower legs. Together, they wrapped it around from below as well. The third piece was the biggest, it covered the entire body. Supplications were written on its edges in a beautiful black script. Hammoudy brought out three bands. Father took one of them and wrapped it around the shroud just above the feet and tied it in a knot. Then they lifted the corpse from the shoulders and Hammoudy pushed the second band with his right hand under the back, and Father caught its other end. They put the corpse down and my father tied the band. They did the same with the third band, which held the edge of the shroud near the head. Father took a deep breath, looked at the shrouded corpse and said out loud: "There is no power save in God."

The dead man looked like a newborn in swaddling clothes. Father prayed as he washed, but he had not said a single word to Hammoudy. They had worked together for years and communicated with each other only through gazes and nods, at one in their rhythms.

Hammoudy went to the corner, where a few coffins were piled up, and gestured to the men to help him bring one to the washing bench. The younger brother helped him carry it. They set it down next to the bench. Father stood at the head of the bench to lift the shrouded man by the shoulders. Hammoudy stood at the other end, ready to lift the feet. Father said: "God help us." That was the signal to start lifting. They lowered him gently into the coffin. Hammoudy went to the garden and brought back a branch from a palm tree. He handed it to my father, who broke it into two pieces. He placed one alongside the right arm between the collar bone and the hand and placed the other at the identical spot on the left side. (Later, my father told me that the branches were supposed to lessen the torture of the grave. At times he would make use of branches of lotus or pomegranate.) He covered the coffin and said to the two men: "May

God have mercy on his soul." This sentence signaled that the ritual was now complete.

The elder brother paid for the shroud and threw in some extra money. Then the two brothers carried the coffin out. Hammoudy helped as well. Father told me to open the door for them. When I returned inside he was returning the bowls to their places—although he kept one out next to the bench. When Hammoudy returned ten minutes later, he filled that bowl with hot water and took out some ground lotus leaves and started to wash and scrub the bench with a sponge. Father then went to the side room and sat down in his chair. I heard his worry beads clicking before they were drowned out by a song from the radio which he'd just turned on. I felt the song was coming from a distant world which was not yet submerged in death as this room had been for the past hour or so.

I was astonished by Father's ability to return to the normal rhythm of life so easily each time after he washed as if nothing had happened. As if he were merely moving from one room to another and leaving death behind. As if death had exited with the coffin and proceeded to the cemetery and life had returned to this place.

When we returned home that evening my mother asked me about my first day on the job with Father. "Good," I said. She was happy and said: "You're a real champ."

But I imagined that death had followed me home. I couldn't stop thinking that everything that Father had bought for us was paid for by death. Even what we ate was paid for by death. When we had dinner that night I watched Father's fingers cut the bread and put food in his mouth. It was hard to believe that these were the same fingers that had rubbed a dead body only a few hours before.

The dead man's face kept gazing at me that night, but he had no eyes, just hollow sockets. I didn't dare tell Mother or Father about the nightmare I kept having that entire summer. The man's face would sometimes disappear and be replaced with the faces of other dead people. Their eye sockets were hollow as well, but he would always return, gazing at me in silence without shutting his eyes.

The faces and bodies of the dead would change, but the rhythm of the washing was fixed. Only rarely would it vary.

Toward the end of that summer they brought in a man who'd been burned to death in an accident at a petrochemical plant. His body was covered with severe burns. The fire had eaten away his skin and discolored all over. Father removed his clothes with great difficulty and poured water on his corpse, but he shrouded and cottoned him without using lotus or camphor or rubbing him down. His relatives were so aghast that they waited outside. I vomited that day and was sick for days. Father wasn't too worried. He said: "Don't worry. You'll get used to it." It wasn't until the following summer that I went back to work with him.

FIVE

"What are you writing?" Father asked when he saw me jotting down notes in a small notebook.

"I'm writing down notes about washing so as not to forget anything."

He laughed: "You think this is school? Don't worry. No exams here."

He said that he'd mastered his profession through practice and without writing a single letter down, as had Hammoudy and all those who had worked with him before. His notebooks were all in his head, written down by the years. But he was quite patient with my many questions and I think was happy to see how serious I was in wanting to know everything about the details and rituals of the profession he wanted me to inherit. I sought his approval and wanted him to know that I, too, wanted to help him as my brother Ammoury had and that I could face death like a man.

I asked him once, just as I'd asked Mother before, why we wash the dead. He said that every dead person will meet with the angels and the people of the afterlife and God Almighty and therefore must be pure and clean. Decomposition must not show on the body, and its odor should be made pleasant. It should be covered so that the hearts of the living be not hardened. I also asked him about the differences between us and the Sunnis in washing. He said they were very minor indeed. Certain details involving the mention of imams and the writing of supplications on the shroud, but nothing major. He said that Christians and Jews may also wash a Muslim if there are no Muslims at hand. The important thing, he added, was to be possessed of noble intentions.

It was absolutely crucial that a man wash a man and that a woman wash a woman. I asked him what if there were no men around. He said a husband may wash his wife, mother, sister, and daughter. A mother may wash her son. I asked him what one should do if there were no camphor or lotus. He said it was acceptable to wash with water alone. "What if there is no water," I asked.

He shook his head and smiled: "Wash with clean sand or dust."

I asked why, and he said that the origin of life is water and dust and if there is no water for ablutions or washing, then pure earth can be used.

I asked whether he ever had to wash someone like that—without water. He said that the *mghaysil* had three water tanks on the roof in case there was a water shortage.

The great majority of bodies that Father washed were intact—except for a young man who had been hit by a speeding car as he crossed the street. When they brought his corpse, it was wrapped in blood-stained nylon. My father put on gloves and told Hammoudy to do the same before they carried the man's body to the bench. I got goose bumps when I saw the body. It looked as if a pack of wolves had attacked it and devoured much of the skin and flesh. Father had once told me that as long as there is a part containing the heart, then one must wash and shroud. I felt that even though he was dead, the man would still feel pain if anyone touched his body. Father poured the water without rubbing or washing with camphor or lotus, but the blood kept flowing from time to time despite the three washes. He used huge quantities of cotton that day to stop the bleeding, but even after he'd shrouded the man, a stain of blood appeared on the right side. My father assured the family that this wouldn't invalidate the shrouding.

SIX

An old man with long white hair and a long white beard wakes me up and says in a voice that seems to come from afar: *Wake up, Jawad, and write down all the names!* I think it very odd that he knows my name. I look at his eyes. They are a strange sky-blue color, set deep into his eye sockets. His face is laced with wrinkles as if he were hundreds of years old. I ask him flatly: *Who are you? What names?* He smiles: *You don't recognize me? Get a pen and paper and write down all the names. Don't forget a single name. They are the names of those whose souls I will pluck tomorrow and whose bodies I will leave for you to purify.* I get out of bed and bring a pen and a notebook and kneel on the ground before him and say: *I'm ready.* He shuts his eyes and starts to recite hundreds of names, and I write down every one. I don't remember how long we have done this, but he opens his eyes after he reads the last name. He takes a deep breath and says in a low voice: *Tomorrow I shall return.* Then he disappears. When I look at the notebook in front of me, I see only one sentence which I've written hundreds of times on each page: *Every soul shall taste death.*

SEVEN

I said nothing to Father about the slight boredom I was experiencing by the end of the first summer. But I told Ammoury, who chastised me for acting like a spoiled baby. "This is not a game," he said. I should grow up and recognize the importance of what Father was doing and why we needed to help him out.

I had gotten used to seeing the dead up close, but hadn't touched a single body throughout that first summer. In the beginning of my second summer, I went back to help out my father. Those hot days passed very slowly, at times with no washing whatsoever. The air conditioner in the side room was no match. After one month, Hammoudy fell sick and couldn't work. For two weeks in July, I had to assume a more active role.

I still remember how cold and strange the first body I helped my father wash and shroud felt. It was an old man in his sixties. His skin was heavily wrinkled and yellowed. He gave off a horrible smell. That day I realized the wisdom of using ground lotus leaves and camphor.

The sight of him reminded me of the fish my mother used to put on the kitchen table to clean before cooking. I was curious to touch the fish's skin but felt a mixture of fascination and disgust afterward. I spent a long time looking at the fish as it lay on its side. With its open mouth and thick lips, its head looked like a human head, crying out, demanding to be returned to the water. The eye, too, was open looking into our eyes. We, who were about to devour it.

The eyes and mouth of the dead man were both shut. He was

asleep and would never wake up again. Father noticed how nervous I was and how hurried and clumsy I was in pouring the water. As if wanting the whole thing to be over. Twice he had to tell me: "Slow down, son! Take it easy!" When we finished I rushed out to the street to catch a breath of fresh air.

EIGHT

He stepped into the classroom confidently, carrying a leather bag out of which he took a stack of drawing pads and a sack full of pencils that he put on the table. He went to the board and wrote in a nice script and big letters: FAN, art. Then he wrote his name in smaller letters: Raid Ismael. He was in his early twenties, with curly black hair and a thick beard. His light green shirt lit up his dark face. When he turned toward us and smiled, most of the students were still in recess mode and hadn't noticed his entrance. He clapped three times to get their attention and said: "Come on, guys. Please. Back to your places. Let's get started." He pointed to his name on the board. "My name is Raid."

At school, sports and arts classes were ignored and we often spent those classes (especially arts) playing soccer, or trying to sneak out to roam around the neighborhood. Some years we would get teachers assigned for arts, other years we wouldn't. Dealing with sports was easier, because all the teacher needed was a few balls and some exercises. Arts, however, was a more challenging subject. Our school didn't have a special arts room, and the administration wasn't keen on providing the necessary material for teachers. Energies and resources were channeled into more "serious" subjects. Thus most arts teachers, if they bothered to show up at all, killed time by chatting with us or letting us do our homework for other classes. Meanwhile, they would read the newspaper or look out the window, asking us to keep it down when we became too noisy.

I had always enjoyed drawing and had started to do a great deal of it during that first summer I worked with father. The hours of waiting for death were long and boring. After I'd exhausted all my questions about death and filled numerous notebooks with notes about the rituals of washing, I started to draw father's face from various angles, capturing him in the washhouse and at home watching TV. He wasn't bothered at all and teased me sometimes: "Isn't that enough? I'm no Saddam Hussein!"

One day, I drew Hammoudy as well. I liked his short spiky hair, wide eyes, and beautiful eyelashes. He liked his portrait so much that he asked to keep it. I offered to draw his portrait on a bigger piece of paper the next day and he was ecstatic. Father and Hammoudy were the only live models I could draw. I filled the notebooks with sketches of the washing bench and the shadows that gathered around it at various hours of the day. I drew the water faucet and tried to show the droplet of water at the moment it was about to fall from the faucet, but I couldn't get it right.

Once, father got very angry when he found out that I was sketching the face of a dead man he'd washed just that morning. He scolded me: "Shame on you! The dead have their sanctity. Draw your father or Hammoudy as much as you want, but leave the dead in peace!"

Flustered, I lied, saying that I had been sketching the face of a relative who had accompanied the dead man and not the dead man himself.

He snatched the notebook from me and pointed to the sketch and said: "Don't lie! Here he is lying on the washing bench!" He ripped the page out and tore it to pieces.

I apologized and never did it again. I felt ashamed and humiliated and went out to the little garden and sat next to the pomegranate tree, tending to my wounds. I turned to a new page and started to sketch the tree and the pomegranates it bore.

Mr. Ismael told us that life is the eternal subject of art and that the world and everything in it are constantly calling out: "Draw me!" He never said that death and the dead were outside the bounds of art. I regret not having asked father what harm there was in drawing the dead. Would it change anything or disturb their eternal sleep?

In addition to his zeal and his seriousness in dealing with art, what distinguished Mr. Ismael was how he treated us as his friends. He never ridiculed us, never dismissed or devalued our opinions when we disagreed with him.

He walked between the rows of desks distributing the drawing pads and pencils while we looked on in disbelief. He asked those who liked drawing to raise their hands and I raised mine high. I looked around. Many others had raised their hands too. He smiled and said: "Marvelous! Picasso, one of the greatest artists of the twentieth century, said: 'Every child is an artist. The challenge is for the artist to stay a child when he grows up!'"

One of the students in the back said: "But we are not children, sir."

There was laughter and Mr. Ismael laughed too and said: "You are young men and not children. The idea is that art allows the child imprisoned inside the adult to come out to play and celebrate the world and its beauty."

He said that art was intimately linked with immortality: a challenge to death and time, a celebration of life. He said that our ancestors in Mesopotamia were the first to pose all these questions in their myths and in the epic of Gilgamesh, and that Iraq was the first and biggest art workshop in the world. In addition to inventing writing and building the first cities and temples, the first works of art and statues had appeared in ancient Iraq during the Sumerian era and now fill museums all over the world. Many still remained buried underground.

He said that we all were inheritors of this great treasure of civilization that enriches our present and future and makes modern Iraqi art so fertile. He asked whether we knew of the Liberty Monument in Liberation Square and the name of the artist who designed it, but we didn't.

"Memorize the name of this man: Jawad Salim," he said.

Mr. Ismael took out an apple. He put his bag and the apple on the table and asked us to draw them in fifteen minutes. Silence reigned except for the lead in our pencils scratching against the surface of the paper and the squeaking of a nearby desk whose occupant kept erasing what he'd just drawn. I started to sketch. I was seated in the third row close to the table. Those who were in the back had to stand up every now and then to look.

Mr. Ismael walked around checking each drawing and making comments. When he got to my desk, he stood and looked for half a minute without saying anything. I'd finished drawing the table, bag, and apple and started to add the shades in the corners and some other tiny details, especially how the sun's rays entered the classroom from the window next to the table and how the bag blocked some of the light, leaving the apple in the shade.

I expected him to criticize me, but he said: "Well done, Jawad. Marvelous! Marvelous!" I was very happy with his approval and praise.

He continued to walk around and announced that ten minutes had passed. Five minutes later, he asked us to stop and put our pencils down. Then he told us to get up and have a look at what the others had drawn without making noise. Of course there was some chatter and some students who pretended to be critics, pointing with their fingers and offering silly comments. I saw one drawing that I thought could compete with mine, but the others were quite ordinary or incomplete.

After ten minutes the teacher asked us to go back to our seats. He asked what we had noticed. Hadi raised his hand.

"Yes, Hadi."

Hadi said, "No one can draw."

Some laughed, but most protested loudly against this destructive criticism. The teacher clapped again to silence everyone and yelled: "Enough!" He reprimanded Hadi, saying: "Everything has its time, but I will not tolerate such disrespect. Each student has drawn the scene from his spot and the same scene appears slightly different from a different angle. Therefore, perspective is very important in drawing."

He asked us to pay attention to the proportionality and size of objects. We shouldn't, for example, draw the bag very tiny and the apple very huge. He said he would show us the best drawing he'd seen. He came toward me and took my pad and returned to the middle of the classroom and stood there.

He raised the pad and said: "Look at your colleague Jawad's drawing. There is attention to proportion and accuracy in capturing details. Well done, Jawad! Marvelous!"

I was filled with joy as everyone looked at me and he returned my pad. He said that he would tell us more the following week about light and shade and their relationship. Our homework assignment was to draw the TV at home.

After class I went to thank him for the pad. He asked whether I'd studied art before. I said I hadn't, but that it was a hobby and I had many notebooks filled with sketches. He said: "You have a strong hand and are talented." I was happy and thanked him.

Mr. Ismael's class became my favorite that year. I waited all week for that one hour. In every class, he would choose one or two drawings and use them to demonstrate strengths and weaknesses. Despite his evenhandedness and the special attention he gave every student, I still felt that he praised me more often. This earned me the jealousy of some of the students. Hadi used to tease me and said once in front of all the students: "Mr. Ismael is a homo and he wants to fuck you!" I was very angry and told him that he was an idiot and was jealous, but he said: "Why, then, does he always talk to you after class?" He kept repeating: "Jawad is a faggot. Jawad is a faggot. Jawad is a faggot." I was furious and we got into a fight, but other students separated us. I swore never to talk to him again and told my friends that they had to choose between being my friends or his. He used to say out loud right before arts class: "Your fucker is coming. Your fucker is coming."

Mr. Ismael noticed that I was sulking that day and asked me what was wrong, but I said nothing to him. I told Ammoury, who said that Hadi was jealous and I should just ignore him.

Mr. Ismael organized several artistic activities at our school, and we were asked to work together in groups to design a wall newspaper, which included literary texts and artwork. We also organized an exhibition which featured the best drawings of the year. He selected two of mine. One was inspired by al-Sayyab's poem "Rain Song," the other was of my father holding his worry beads. The drawings were hung on a wall close to the principal's office, and the names and sections of students were written under them. The exhibition went on for a month and I was happy to see my name in big letters next to my drawings and to see students and teachers standing before them.

One day after class Mr. Ismael asked me: "What do you want to be when you grow up, Jawad?"

Without hesitation I said: "Jawad Salim."

He laughed and patted my shoulder saying: "An artist. Why not? You can study at the academy, but you must keep to your drawing and never stop."

I answered: "Of course, Sir."

At the end of the year he asked me to go to his office after class and to bring my backpack along. The last part sounded odd. When I got there he asked me to sit down on the chair in front of his desk. He repeated what he'd told me throughout the year about my talent and unique eye. He said I was the best student in all of his classes, better even than those who were older. He added that talent was important, but it was not sufficient by itself and had to be augmented by constant practice and study.

He opened the drawer and took out two pads of the same sort he had given us at the beginning of the year. He took a plastic sack out of his leather bag and put it on his desk. He asked me to take out what was inside. I did and there was a midsize box of watercolors with two brushes and a set of pastels. I was delighted by the surprise and a bit shy. I didn't know what to say except a soft "thank you." He said that it was a gift to encourage me to develop my abilities. I thanked him again and told him that his was my favorite class and that I'd learned so much.

"You deserve much more, Jawad," he said. "You will not be Jawad Salim, but you can be a fabulous Iraqi artist one day." He looked at his watch and said that he had to go to another class. We shook hands warmly and I put his precious gift in my bag. I thanked him again and we said goodbye.

After our last class before the summer break I waited for the other students to leave, especially Hadi, and then gave Mr. Ismael a gift. It was a profile of his face I'd worked on for weeks until I got the best version possible. I wrote on the back: *To the best teacher ever. From your grateful student Jawad Kazim.* He was very happy as he looked at it. He said he would cherish it and frame it. He shook my hands warmly and patted me on the shoulder. He reminded me to keep drawing and said that he was looking forward to seeing what I would draw during the summer.

During the summer I filled the two pads with drawings after having practiced using watercolors on ordinary paper. I liked to draw with pastel too, but I focused on strengthening my hand with the brush. For the first time ever I found myself impatiently waiting for the break to end so I could show Mr. Ismael my new drawings.

On the first day of school I looked at the rosters of students and teachers and at the schedules posted on the wall next to the administration offices. His name did not appear anywhere and there was an X instead of his name next to "Arts." My heart sank and I asked the assistant principal about him. He said that Mr. Ismael had been called up for military service and that they'd assign a new teacher.

When it was time for arts class on Thursday, the vice principal came into our classroom and said: "No arts. You can leave." I inquired about the new teacher. He said: "There is no new teacher." I asked why. He said: "No idea, son."

The arts class became a free hour during which students had fun playing and running around, but for me it was impossible to fill that void with anything. I never studied art with any other teacher after that and never had any further formal training until I entered the Academy of Fine Arts five years later. One month after the start of that academic year in 1980, the war with Iran started. I always wondered about Mr. Ismael's fate as I watched the footage of fierce battles on TV. I asked other teachers whether they'd heard anything about him, but no one knew anything.

NINE

She was all in black. I was late for my art history class that morning because I had decided to sleep an extra fifteen minutes past the alarm. The professor was strict about attendance and wouldn't allow anyone who was more than ten minutes late to enter. Students called him "The Englishman" because of his obsession with time and because of the fluency and excessive—and somewhat pretentious—accuracy with which he pronounced various English terms. I was panting when I quietly opened the door to the lecture hall. I thought maybe he'd forgive me, but he shook his index finger and pointed to his watch and gestured to me to close the door. I did and walked to the kiosk outside the academy and bought a copy of *al-Jumhuriyya*. I read the headlines on my way to the cafeteria. Nothing new except military communiqués and constant victories over the enemy. I folded it and put it with my books. I went to the cafeteria, because I hadn't had time to have breakfast at home. I bought a white cheese sandwich and a cup of tea.

There were no seats inside but it was warm so I went outside and found an empty bench near the theater department. A group of theater students wearing black were sitting around a palm tree. I sat down and began to devour my sandwich while reading the sports page as usual. My favorite soccer team, al-Zawra', had lost two of its stars because they were called to the national team, which was preparing for the Asia Tournament. Al-Zawra's performance had started to decline, and it had lost the previous day's away match against Najaf, even though Najaf's team was in last place.

I turned to the culture pages. There was a feeble poem about the war and under it an interview with an arts critic. I saw a long article about the *Arabian Nights* and the Arabic literary tradition and how both had influenced Latin American writers. I heard someone clap. It was one of the theater professors who was a famous experimental director. He had a cloud of white hair and was wearing jeans, a white shirt, and sunglasses. He asked the students around the palm tree to pay attention.

I went back to the article. It was discussing Borges's fascination with the East and a story he'd written about Averroes, but I couldn't concentrate. I heard the professor again explaining the exercise they were about to begin. He asked three of the students to sit on the ground and imagine themselves on a sinking boat and to act out their predicament without words. He asked the others to watch. One of the students asked what kind of boat it should be and the professor answered: "Whatever you like, as long as it sinks." Most of them laughed.

I was intrigued, so I got up and sat on a closer bench to watch, but kept a reasonable distance so as not to be annoying. The professor called out three names and asked them to be the first to perform. Reem was one of them. She squatted on the ground and held her knees with her arms and looked to the professor awaiting his signal. She was wearing baggy black pants and a black cotton shirt with an open neck and long sleeves she'd folded back a few times so that her arms were showing. Her jet-black hair was tied back. The professor signaled for the sinking to begin.

Later I saw her standing in line at the cafeteria. She'd changed and was wearing a gray skirt with a white shirt. I approached her and said, "I wanted to save you from drowning, but I can't swim."

She turned toward me with a scowl and asked very seriously: "Excuse me. Come again?"

"The exercise. This morning? Drowning . . . I was sitting there and saw you drowning."

She laughed and said: "Oh, yes. Thank you for your gallantry, but it's useless if you can't swim."

"Intentions don't matter?"

"Yes, of course. Intentions are crucial."

Then she introduced herself: "Reem, theater."

I said: "Delighted. Jawad. Arts."

Her eyes were pitch-black and gleamed with confidence as she spoke somewhat slowly. Her eyelashes were thick, her eyebrows carefully plucked. She was wearing light makeup. She bought crackers and a cup of tea with milk and offered to buy me something in appreciation of my noble intentions. I thanked her but I had to leave for a class. I noticed the gold ring on her left hand as she paid and felt a pang in my heart. Damn! She's married. All this beauty for another man who waits for her at the end of the day.

"Some other time then," she said.

We said goodbye and I headed to the door. We exchanged smiles. I could train myself, I determined, to be just friends with a woman.

I saw her again a week later on the sidewalk outside the academy. She was getting into a beautiful blue car with tinted windows. The driver was a man, probably her husband, wearing sunglasses. I caught only his black moustache. Then she disappeared and I didn't see her again that year. One day I saw a friend I'd seen her with and asked about Reem's disappearance. She said that Reem had dropped out for personal reasons, but she refused to say more. I wondered whether Reem was ill. I asked other students in the theater department and heard a rumor that her husband had forced her to drop out.

TEN

I remembered how my father shook his head when he was certain that I wanted to make the Academy of Fine Arts my first choice. My average score in the countrywide baccalaureate exam was 87.7 percent. That would probably guarantee acceptance in the engineering departments at al-Mustansiriyya University and other universities in the provinces, or in fields such as literature or the sciences if I made these my top choices.

He asked me sarcastically: "So what will you be after you finish? An arts teacher?"

I answered: "Maybe. What's wrong with that, anyway? Is teaching shameful? There are other types of work as well."

He handed back the list and repeated a favorite sentence: "One has to look out for one's livelihood, son!" And after a heavy silence: "Even if you don't want to work with me, at least study something useful for yourself and others. Something good!"

I wasn't surprised, but the episode saddened me. He never forgave me for straying from the path and favoring art over the useful profession he had inherited from his ancestors. I folded the sheet of paper without saying anything. Mother, who was sitting at the other end of the couch, tried, as usual, to lighten the mood: "Great things are awaiting Jawad and he deserves the best. Good luck, son."

Father gave her a silent look and then went back to nursing his cup of tea.

ELEVEN

"Pythagoras says that there is music in stone."

So began Professor Isam al-Janabi's first lecture on the history of sculpture. I still remember the details clearly. He added that Goethe appropriated this idea and used it in a remark about architecture as frozen music. Professor Isam al-Janabi's style in his lectures about art and life seemed like poetry to me. He was adept at using quotations to crystallize the subjects of his lectures or illustrate the ideas he was explaining to us. He once quoted Picasso: "Art is the lie that represents truth." The images and slides he used gave his lectures an additional dimension and set them apart from the dry and boring styles of the other professors.

He was almost fifty. He'd been to Italy a few years before, after completing his graduate studies. He was a famous artist, well known throughout the Arab world, and had had numerous exhibitions. He also published occasional critical essays in newspapers and journals about art history. His style of dress was stereotypically bohemian. His long curly hair was the longest among students and professors. He had a bushy moustache and long beard whose white fringes he used to stroke a lot.

He asked for help closing the shades for the slide show. I was sitting in the back of the darkened lecture hall, one of thirty-some students. I took out my notebook and prepared to jot down notes. Speaking without notes, he took us on a panoramic journey through the history of sculpture.

He was collecting his papers and putting them in his bag after class when I approached him to ask about Giacometti. He had showed us images of some of Giacometti's works which fascinated me, especially one entitled *Man Walking*. He smiled as he put his bag over his shoulder and asked, "What in particular do you like about him?"

I was a bit flustered, because I'd never reflected on my reasons for loving certain works of art. Beauty would simply and suddenly hit me in the gut. I hesitated, then said, "I don't know exactly, but I felt that the man he sculpted was sad and isolated."

Professor Isam al-Janabi smiled, and his eyes glittered. "Bravo. Many critics say that his works express an existentialist attitude toward the emptiness and meaninglessness of life." He said the last sentence in standard Arabic and in a different tone. Then he added: "Remind me of your name again?"

"Jawad," I said.

"Of course you loved him, Jawad. How could you not?"

We left the lecture hall together and continued our conversation about Giacometti and abstract sculpture until we reached his office. He asked me to come in. Stacks of papers, books, and clippings were piled on his desk and chair. The shelves were piled to the ceiling with books. He put his bag on his desk, then gathered the pile of manuscripts and newspapers from a chair so I could sit. I looked at the books. Most of them were in Arabic and English, but there were some titles in Italian. A huge black-and-white poster of Giacometti covered what was left of the wall. In the picture, Giacometti was carrying one of his tiny statues and walking between two thin large ones. I was taken by the poster, and Professor Isam al-Janabi noticed my reaction.

He looked at it as if seeing it for the first time: "Ah, here is your friend Giacometti in his studio." Then he asked me about my background and interests, listening intently to everything I had to say. He, too, had come from a poor family. His father worked at a paper mill and wanted him to be an engineer, not an artist.

I asked whether he'd met Giacometti. He said he hadn't, because Giacometti died years before he had gone to Europe. He got out of his chair and looked for something on the shelves. After half a minute, he reached up and plucked a book from one of the top shelves. It was a big book with Giacometti's name written in a big font on the cover. He blew the dust away and gave it to me, saying it contained all of Giacometti's works and I could borrow it, provided I took good care of it. I was very happy. He looked at his watch and said that he had a lecture in a few minutes. I apologized and thanked him for his time. We shook hands and said goodbye.

I left his office and headed to the library to use the dictionary to help me understand the English texts and captions accompanying the images. I sat leafing through the book fondly, reading all about Giacometti's life. I was fascinated by his work and wanted to know its secrets, so I started looking at his family photos wanting to know everything about him as if he'd become a relative. I learned that he was born in 1901 in Switzerland and died in 1966 after living through two world wars. Perhaps that explained the sadness in his works. He had studied in Paris with Bourdelle, who had worked with Rodin, but his work was so distinct that it was difficult to categorize. His statues were conspicuously thin, as if they were threads or thin mummies exhumed out of tombs. The body was always naked and with minimal features. Some works were of a hand waving alone without a body. Humans, in Giacometti's world, be they men or women, appeared sad and lonely, with no clear features, emerging from the unknown and striding toward it.

There was one page in the book that had quotations by Giacometti. One of them stayed with me. He said that what he'd wanted to sculpt was not man but the shadow he leaves behind.

TWELVE

The first week of my fourth year at the academy I saw Reem sitting on a bench near the theater department all in black and wearing sunglasses. I approached her and said hello. She greeted me amicably but apologized for not recognizing or remembering me. I reminded her of my name and my silly joke about trying to save her from drowning after that exercise and of our short conversation at the cafeteria. I asked her about the black she was wearing. She said that her ex-husband had died two months before. I offered my condolences. She thanked me and smiled, saying that he was an officer and had died on the front line. I mentioned that my brother was a martyr, too. I didn't want to burden her so I didn't ask why she'd been away for so long, but I asked whether she was back in school. She nodded with a smile. Death had brought her back to me.

THIRTEEN

One morning I surprised Reem with a question I'd been meaning to ask but had hesitated to pose: "Did you love him a lot?"

"Who?"

I found it strange that she didn't realize I meant her ex-husband. "The deceased."

She turned to me and looked at me with her magic eyes. We were sitting next to each other under the palm tree she loved. Then she looked straight ahead without saying a word. I feared that I'd hurt her feelings or reopened wounds that had yet to heal, so I said "I'm sorry. Didn't mean to . . . "

She smiled and said, "No, it's not a problem. It's a sensitive subject. I will answer you when I can trust you more."

"And when will that be?"

"Don't rush."

After that day I was careful not to bring up her marriage again. Two months later we were sitting at the cafeteria of the British Council near the academy. She asked me about my relationship with my father. I told her about my clashes with him, that he was disappointed in me because I had decided not to follow in his footsteps and insisted on studying art, which he thought was a waste of time.

She said that her father never paid any attention to what she did or wanted to do. "I wish he'd insisted I study one thing or even objected to my studying at the academy. I would've interpreted that as a sign that he cared or loved me. But he was always busy with his business and I rarely saw him. Only his wife, who was another of his profitable deals, could compete for the attention he usually devoted to his business. He married her after my mother passed away. After moving in with us, she turned my life into hell and fought me in every way possible. So marriage was my only escape.

"I didn't love my husband, but I hoped that living with him would lead to another kind of love. I'd fallen in love with a young man who lived on our street when I was in high school, but I later realized that it wasn't a serious or meaningful relationship. We were both young and spoke on the phone a great deal, whispering and whatnot. We met every now and then whenever it was possible. It withered away when he moved with his family to al-Sayyidiyya. It was quite far and he didn't have a car. Our nocturnal chats became less frequent and the whole thing just died.

"During the summer vacation right before I entered the academy, one of my relatives asked for my hand. I'd seen him two or three times at weddings. He had studied engineering and then became a lieutenant in the Republican Guards. He got two medals for bravery during the war. He'd seen me once leaving high school and offered to drive me home. I thanked him politely but refused his offer. He later confessed that it wasn't a coincidence at all and that he had approached me so as to test the waters. Although I never believed in traditional marriage, my only goal was to free myself from my stepmother, and I came to the conclusion that I had no choice but to compromise.

"Ayad was handsome. He was pleasant during the initial visits. Throughout our engagement he would come every three weeks during his leaves from the army. He was very gentle and understanding at first and promised that I could complete my studies and be independent. I liked his maturity, especially when I informed him that I didn't want to have kids until after my studies. He agreed and said that he would want to be in Baghdad, not on the front, when his children were born so he could raise them himself. It seemed that the war would go on for another two or three years anyway.

"Since living alone was impossible financially and socially, I decided that marriage was the best choice among a set of bad options. My father didn't care that much. He said that Ayad was successful and established financially and that would guarantee me a secure future. I felt he was talking about one of those profitable deals he was so good at. As for my stepmother, she didn't even bother to hide how happy she was to be getting rid of me.

"The wedding took place at the Sheraton, and our honeymoon was one week at the Habbaniyya Lake Resort. He went back to the front line afterward and I went to our little nest, which he'd bought in Zayyuna, next to the Fashion House. His salary was excellent, but he'd also inherited money from his father, who'd died two years before in a car accident.

"Our problems started during his second leave, when I realized that the polite Ayad was a mountain hiding a volcano. It was very easy for it to pour lava on everything and everyone around. It was never easy to predict what would set the volcano off. The first eruption was because my cooking failed to rise to his standards. I wasn't a great cook, but I tried earnestly and enlisted the help of my maternal aunt. I hand-copied my grandmother's famous recipes to secure his satisfaction. He said that even the army food was better than my cooking. I apologized and promised to improve with practice. I had warned him when we were engaged that I was not a good cook, but he'd said that he was used to army food and we'd cook together. His sweet talk during our engagement was like the courting of political parties before they assume power.

"He used to always apologize and shower me with kisses, especially on my hands, after hitting me. He used to buy me gifts and promise that he would never lift his hand against me again and that it was the last time. But every time was the last time. In one of his fits of rage, he broke my arm. The pain was so excruciating he took me to the Tawari' Hospital at night and told them that I'd tripped and fallen down the stairs. I kept silent, but my tears were obvious. I sensed that the resident doctor suspected my husband's story, but all he did was look at him suspiciously. I thought about screaming that he had hit me. But who was going to believe that a valiant officer who had been awarded three medals by the president would harm his own wife?

"After that, I decided to move back to my father's house. Ayad apologized and pleaded, but I'd heard it all before.

"I tried to feel some sadness when Ayad died, but I couldn't. I was so relieved that I felt guilty for that. My tears at the funeral were genuine, but I was crying for myself and all the years of my life that had died. I visit Ayad's mother sometimes. She's a kind person. She knew how cruel he was and understood my suffering. But she still keeps a framed photo of him on her TV: Ayad accepting a medal from Saddam Hussein."

FOURTEEN

She was cautious with me at the outset of our friendship. More than once she made me feel that I had to slow down. I learned to be patient, to crawl into her heart instead of storming it impulsively.

With time, friendship turned into something more intense. We didn't talk about what we felt precisely, but our silent gazes meeting for a few seconds were eloquent. When we walked or sat together, I felt the air between us grow moist. Often I drew her and gave her my sketches. She would thank me shyly and say, "Is there no one else for you to draw? No other subject?" I would answer, "No, no one but you."

I once told her that I would love to sculpt her.

"And the price?"

"For free. A gift. But, you have to . . . you know. For it to be exact." Then I gestured with my hands that she would have to get naked.

She laughed out loud: "No way. That's an old trick. A tree could grow on your head and I would still not allow you."

"Alas, had you said 'When a tree grows on your head, then I will allow you,' I would have at least tried to plant one there."

She laughed, "Anyway, if your style is abstract as you claim, why do you need a model?"

"Inspiration, my dear colleague."

"Oh, how collegial of you!"

Suddenly, three months later, she invited me to have lunch at her house. I asked her who would be there.

"Why? Are you afraid?"

I laughed. "No, but am I not allowed to ask?"

"My father is at work and his wife is on a trip to Mosul. Do you want to invite anyone else?"

"No, the two of us will do."

It wasn't the first time we'd been alone in her car. We had occasionally gone to plays together, and she would drive me home afterward. But this was the first time I was going to her house or anywhere knowing that we would be by ourselves.

The house was in al-Jadiriyya, huge and elegant. She let me in through the kitchen door and I followed her along a corridor to the guest room. She asked me to make myself at home while she heated the food. I asked whether she needed any help. "No, you are my guest," she said. She offered me a drink, but I declined. She smiled and left me contemplating the extravagant furniture and precious Persian carpets.

She returned ten minutes later carrying a tablecloth and plates with silverware. She spread the white tablecloth and then set plates down in front of two of the eight chairs. One was at the head of the table and the other right next to it so that we would occupy a corner. I wasn't used to all these elaborate preparations for a meal. I followed her into the kitchen. She laughed: "Where are you going?"

"It's not right. I have to help you."

She scooped the yellow rice she'd warmed into a big dish and asked me to carry it. It was mixed with almonds, raisins, and pieces of chicken. The smell of saffron filled the air. I took the dish and put it on the table. When I went back to the kitchen she pointed to a big salad bowl she'd taken out of the fridge. "That one, too, please." She followed me carrying a tray that had two bottles of Pepsi, two glasses, and some bread. We sat down to eat.

I loved to watch her do anything, no matter how mundane or casual. I loved to watch her eat. The food was good, and I asked who should be praised. She said the maid, an experienced cook, came three times a week. I asked about her battles with her stepmother. She said that peace now prevailed, because her father had remodeled the house after she had moved back in. He had built an additional room on the second floor. A living room next to her bedroom served as an office and a TV room. She had her own bathroom, so she came downstairs only to eat, and she rarely had to deal with her stepmother. She said, as she smiled shyly, that she would show me what she called her private wing after lunch. I interpreted this as an encouraging sign.

After we finished eating I thanked her and we took the dishes back to the kitchen. She said I could wash my hands in the bath room upstairs. We went up the stairs, which were made of marble tiles and led to a wooden door. She opened it and I closed it behind us. The first door on the left was the bathroom. She opened the door and showed me in, saying she was going to fetch a towel. Her bathroom was bigger than my bedroom. The walls and floor were tiled in light blue. The floor was covered with tiny dark blue rugs. There was a tub behind a see-through curtain. The oval basin was sky-blue.

I turned the faucet knobs, trying to find the right combination of cold and hot water. I took the yellow bar of soap and lathered my hands and mouth. I gargled and rinsed my mouth and hands and then shut the faucet.

She came in and handed me a white towel.

I took the towel with my left hand and put my right hand on her left. She didn't pull away. I told her: "I want to wash your hands."

She laughed: "What? Why?"

I pulled her gently to the basin and turned the faucet on again. I put the new towel over the old one, which was on the bar to the right of the basin. I held both of her hands and put them under the water. She didn't say a word. I took the soap and lathered her right hand carefully, first the knuckles, then the palm, and then I placed each one of her fingers between my thumb and index finger and rubbed them. I did the same with her left hand and then rinsed them both with water before shutting the faucet. She was looking at me the whole time, smiling. I took the towel and dried both of her hands. After I put the towel back on the bar, I held her hands and looked into her eyes. She smiled and said "Thank you" in a hushed voice.

I pulled her toward me and moved my face closer to hers, but she pulled away. I was disappointed, but then she said, "Let me wash my mouth first." She laughed and added, "You forgot to wash it! Go and wait for me. I'll be there right away."

I stood outside the bathroom watching her wash her mouth. She saw me looking at her in the mirror and smiled. She dried her mouth with the towel. She opened the cupboard and took out some lipstick and put a touch of her favorite pink on her lips. She came out of the bathroom, shut the door behind her, and leaned on the wall next to it, just a few steps from me. I approached and stood close to her. Looking at her lips, I leaned over. She closed her eyes and I lightly grazed her lips with mine. Then again. I kissed the right edge of her lips. My mouth slipped toward her right cheek. I moved to her neck. I put my arms around her waist. She sighed and leaned her head back. I felt her hands on my shoulders. I kissed her neck and inhaled that jasmine perfume which had so dizzied me for months.

I encircled her neck with my kisses, then my mouth climbed, kiss by kiss, to her chin. I trapped her upper lip between my lips. She parted her lips and our tongues met. Her thighs had moved closer to my body, and she must have felt my erection. I put my right hand on her breast and tried to unbutton her shirt, but she held my hand and lowered it. She pushed me away gently without saying anything and then walked toward a door at the end of the corridor. I followed her.

Her bedroom was huge. The walls were white and the floor was covered with Persian carpets. There was a medium-size bed with white sheets. The wall above it had a huge black-and-white photo of a table in a café with a closed book and an empty cup of coffee on it—it looked European. The left side of the room had a huge mirror behind a table and a chair. Next to them was a chest made of Indian oak.

She stood by the bed and then turned toward me. She was wearing a white shirt and a gray skirt which barely covered her knees. I approached her and kissed her with more confidence this time. She put her arms around me. I started to unbutton her white shirt and saw her white bra hiding her full breasts. I moved the shirt away to kiss her left shoulder and then kissed her upper arm. She started kissing my neck and I felt fire in my bones.

I went back to her shoulder and moved her bra strap aside to kiss her shoulder again. Then I moved down to the slopes of her left breast. I could smell her perfume again. I removed her shirt and tossed it on the bed. I took her in my arms, kissed her neck again and fumbled with her bra. She laughed and undid it herself and tossed it on the floor. She started to unbutton my shirt as I kissed her pear-shaped breasts and erect nipples. She took off my shirt and let it fall to the floor. She took off her shoes and kicked them aside. I did the same and bent down to quickly remove my socks. I found my mouth right in front of her navel so I kissed it, and found that she was ticklish. We peeled each other piece by piece until all she wore were her black panties. These she grasped with both hands and lowered to her feet. Her pubic hair was shaved. I I took off my white underpants. I was very hard. Naked now except for the gold chain around her neck with her name engraved on it, she lay on the bed sideways.

I knelt and started kissing her knees and then made my way up her left thigh with my lips all the way to her hip, her tummy, and her navel again to tickle her. She giggled and put her fingers through my hair. I climbed on top of her and took her left nipple between my lips. My tongue circled around it a few times before moving to the right. She was sighing and moving under me like a wave. My tongue climbed to her neck and mouth. She kissed me, open-mouthed. I bit her lower lip and my tongue wandered inside her mouth. I went down again to her breasts and nipples and then her navel and kissed her right below it. She had parted her thighs a bit. I surrounded them with my arms and gently kissed her soft inner thighs. Her sighs intensified. I kissed in between. She tasted like the sea. I kept plowing with my tongue and she kept rising in waves until her body overflowed.

Everything quieted down afterward for a minute and my head rested on her thigh. She pulled me up by the hand and I was on top again. She hugged and kissed me and then clasped her legs around me. I entered her looking deep into her large eyes. I kept reentering her body in a rising tempo until I felt I was about to flood. A sweet silence reigned afterward.

I loved her self-confidence and the way she stood there and put her hand on her hip saying: "So, you want to sculpt me now?"

FIFTEEN

I'm sitting alone, watching TV and flipping the channels, but they are all blank. No sound or image. Whiteness, silent whiteness, covers everything. I punch the TV with my fist a few times to no avail. I keep flipping through the channels in search of something that might relieve my insomnia and entertain me a bit. I find only one channel working.

There, five hooded men stand around a sixth, who kneels and wears an orange work suit. A black bag shrouds his head. Four men hold their weapons while their leader reads the execution verdict to the kneeling prisoner. The leader pauses and looks at me, warning: *You better change the channel, because what you will soon see will terrify you and you're not a man.* He goes back to reading from the piece of paper. When he finishes, he folds the paper and puts it in his pocket. One of the hooded men standing behind him hands him a sword. The leader lifts the black bag from the head of the kneeling man, who starts to weep like a child. The leader holds the man's blond hair and tilts his head to the left. He lifts the sword and beheads him with a single blow while intoning: *God is great. God is great.*

I feel nauseated and turn off the TV, but blood flows from the screen, covering everything around me in red.

SIXTEEN

I was startled as I uncovered the face of one of the men I washed yesterday. He looked exactly like a dear friend of mine who'd died years ago. The same rectangular features, high cheek bones, and long nose. The skin and eyes were coffee brown. His eyes were shut, of course. Their sockets were somewhat hollow. The thick eyebrows looked as if they were about to shake hands. *But,* I said to myself, *I've already seen him dead in my own arms once before.* The name on the paper was Muhsin. The distinguishing mark that this person, who looked so much like my friend, had acquired was a bullet hole in the middle of his forehead. It looked like a period which had put an end to the sentence of his life. One of the men who brought him said that he was a shop owner and was killed in a robbery. *Thank God,* I thought. *It's not a sectarian killing. But does it matter to the dead how and why they die? Theft, greed, hatred, or sectarianism? We, who are waiting in line for our turn, keep mulling over death, but the dead person just dies and is indifferent.*

I asked them if they were from al-Samawa. Perhaps he was one of Basim's relatives. One of them asked if something was wrong. "No, nothing. It's just that the deceased looks exactly like a dear friend of mine from al-Samawa and I thought they might be related." He answered with the usual cliché: "God creates forty identical faces."

Basim and I had become close friends during my military service. Without contacts and favors that could get you a posting close to your family, a soldier's fate was like a throw of the dice. After two months of grueling training, the hand of coincidence, or absurdity, landed me in southern Iraq. I was ordered to report to a small unit in al-Samawa, away from Baghdad and everything I'd ever known. The unit was an antiaircraft missile unit temporarily stationed at the al-Samawa cement plant. It was 270 kilometers south of Baghdad, halfway to Basra. The trip took three hours by car.

I was far away from everything, but contrary to my expectations, the distance wasn't a bad thing at all. I missed Reem, of course, and there was no way to contact her. Army life was not easy, but our commanding officer was a kind and easygoing man, and we didn't have many duties. The cement factory had been looted after the 1991 war. After my first leave, I returned to the unit from Baghdad with lots of books to kill the time. I also brought sketchbooks and a tiny radio to listen to music and the news at night. There was a TV in our unit, and we could watch the Baghdad channels and sometimes Kuwaiti TV, but the transmission was weak and I preferred the radio. I didn't miss Baghdad that much. I loved the serenity of the local landscape. I spent most of my time reading, drawing, and contemplating. That's why Basim called me "the intellectual" and always addressed me as "Professor Jawad."

I rediscovered the beauty of stars at night. I never realized that so many of them could crowd the sky. I used to love gazing at them as a child when we slept on the roof during the summer. This is what happens to city people when we are far from our false glitter. I found myself shepherding the stars every night.

It was there that I met Basim. I didn't know it at first, but he would become the star that lit the place for me. He was from al-Samawa and would ask the C.O., Lieutenant Ahmad, for permission to go downtown Thursday evening and return on Friday night. The C.O. would approve, especially since Basim used to get us things we needed, cigarettes, tea, and sugar. The army's supply system was irregular and less efficient than it had been in the 1980s. Basim's father, Hajj Muhammad al-Sudani, was rich and owned a few shops at the al-Samawa suq. Basim had studied history at al-Basra University. He had a great sense of humor and was full of curiosity and joie de vivre. You heard his laughter everywhere he went.

He used to tease me for being a city boy who knew nothing about the desert, for knowing only about the capital. More than once during those first few weeks he invited me to be a guest at his family's home, but I used to thank him and decline. After he repeated the invitation a few times, I realized that he was sincere, so I finally agreed. He promised me a tour of the town and a visit to the remains of the ancient city of al-Warkaa close by. Basim was fascinated by the local history and landscape and took pride in them. He told me about Lake Sawa. I'd seen the name in geography books, but I knew little about it. He took me there in his car during the first month of my service.

At first, on our way there, I did not see the blue and thought we were lost. How could a lake exist amid all this desert? I couldn't see anything on the horizon, but he said that it was difficult to see from a distance, because the lake was five meters above its surroundings and it had a naturally formed wall of gypsum. There was no river feeding it. Its only source was water from deep below the ground. Basim said that it was the same spring from which the water had burst forth when the flood covered the earth in Noah's time. Then the water receded and what was left became Sawa.

"Did you read that in history books at al-Basra University?" I joked.

"Popular history has its own truth," he said. "You're just jealous because Baghdad has no lake."

"The Tigris is more than enough for Baghdad," I said.

He told me that Sawa was the only lake in the world fed entirely by groundwater. It was mentioned in Yaqut al-Hamawi's *Encyclopedia of Cities* and dated back to pre-Islamic times. An ancient city there, Ales, had been an encampment for the Persians. During the Islamic conquests, the Persians and Arab tribes had fought nearby. Sawa was also mentioned in the historical archives of the Ottomans. During their era, it was situated at the al-Atshan River, before a massive flood changed its course in 1700. So even rivers change course. I was a river trying, perhaps in vain, not to flow where the map wanted it to go.

Basim turned off the paved road to the right and drove on a gravel road for five minutes before stopping. He opened the door and said, "Come, Mr. Intellectual, you will thank me forever for introducing you to Sawa."

I got out and went around the car and walked by his side. The sun was about to drop to the horizon and was clad in orange. I noticed that the sky near the horizon was bluer. The road we were walking on sloped and I could see the calm surface of the lake. We stood at the edge.

"Have you ever seen anything like it?" he said.

The lake's beauty was gripping. Its balmy blue was therapeutic, especially for a soul thirsting in the harshness of the desert day and night. Its shore was covered with calcifications that looked like cauliflowers with cavities carved by the salts that filled the lake's waters forming a wall on all sides.

I asked Basim about the fish in the lake. He said it had only one kind, and it was not edible. We squatted and I extended my hand to dip it in the water. It was very cold, as cold as the water I applied now to the body of this man who looked like Basim's twin. I felt guilty. *Here I am washing a dead man's body while my thoughts are wandering in the fissures of my memory. Did father do this as well, or did he focus on his rituals all day long? Is that possible? Here I am, carrying them out in a semimechanical way.*

We used to escape to the lake whenever we had a chance, to sit on its shore and chat. Once, while we were driving around in Basim's car, I saw gutted buildings near the lake. He called them tourist relics. In the late 1980s, the Ministry of Tourism had built a number of apartments and a restaurant in an effort to encourage tourism in the area. The spot became a mecca for family and school trips, but the place was looted and abandoned after the 1991 war. I asked him to take me there. The sight was sad. Nothing was left except the concrete skeletons of the apartment buildings that had been built steep to provide a lake view. They looked like fossils of mythic animals crouched at the lake's feet.

American fighter jets hovered over our unit all the time. We heard in the news about antiaircraft batteries being bombed after the no-fly zone was imposed in northern and southern Iraq after 1992. The no-fly zone was supposed to prevent the regime from oppressing citizens, but these fighter jets would kill innocent civilians and even herders. I never knew whether it was out of sheer idiocy, or whether it was a game, using Iraqis for target practice. Our C.O. stressed that we should ignore the jets and try not to incite the enemy. We were not to lock onto a target and give the pilot a pretext to attack us. Soldiers were ordered to maintain a defensive posture and respond only if attacked. This is how we had many months of peace.

We were awakened at dawn one day by the sound of a massive explosion which shook the factory (as we called our unit). Two more explosions followed. Then we heard the sounds of rocks and pebbles falling on the ceilings and windows and the whizzing of a fighter jet overhead. I got out of bed, quickly put on my uniform, boots, and helmet, and darted outside with the others. I remembered that Basim had been assigned to the night guard shift outside the southern building near the missile battery. Thinking of him, I felt a lump in my throat.

The bombing had caused a storm of dust, some of which got into my eyes and mouth. Shards were scattered in the open space between the two buildings. I could smell gunpowder. Everyone was running toward the southern building, which was about a hundred meters from the main building. The entire building and its tin plank roof had been destroyed, leaving only one of its four columns intact. There was chaos. Some soldiers were trying to lift the tangle of metal and gray blocks to look for survivors under the debris.

I went around the rubble of the building to look for Basim. I used to ridicule those who claimed, before some terrible or painful event took place, "I felt it in my heart." But as I ran toward the back of the building, I felt my heart as a deep well into which stones from every direction began to rain. The branches of the tree next to the missile battery had caught fire. The truck with missiles mounted on it was now a mass of rising flames. Some soldiers were trying to put the fire out with dirt and fire extinguishers. Pieces of metal were scattered about. I spotted a body twenty meters to my right and ran toward it.

He had been thrown onto his stomach, but I recognized his hair. His weapon was three or four meters away. I screamed his name as I ran, but he didn't move. His left arm was twisted backward in a strange position and looked like it had snapped. I knelt next to him and held him by the shoulders as I turned him over on his side. He felt heavy, unresponsive. His coffee eyes were wide open, looking upward. Blood seeping out of his nose and the side of his mouth had covered his moustache. I called his name again and put my ear to his chest but could hear only my own breathing and the screams of others. I lifted my head and held his hand and felt his wrist for a pulse. Nothing. I closed his eyes, kissed his forehead, and took him in my arms. I don't remember how long I stayed there sobbing by his side.

Basim was one of six soldiers who died that day. In the evening I accompanied his body in a military vehicle. The C.O. had asked me to inform his family of his death. I asked the C.O. for permission also to go to al-Samawa to attend the first day of the funeral and he agreed.

I had met Basim's father twice before. His first words were "There is no power save in God." Then he asked: "Did he suffer?"

I answered that he hadn't, though I wasn't sure. Six or seven minutes had passed between the time of the explosion and when I found him.

The southern building was never repaired or rebuilt. The rubble was shoveled into a mound and just left there.

I put a swab of cotton into the hole the bullet had bored in the man's forehead and another swab into his nostrils. I had already put swabs between his buttocks and inside his anus. I prepared to shroud him.

SEVENTEEN

In the winter of 2003 it seemed that, once again, war was coming. My mother asked Father, "What are we going to do? Are we staying in Baghdad?"

He said: "Where else would we go? If God wants to end our lives, he will do so here. This is not the first war, but I sure hope it will be the last one. Enough."

She asked me more than once, as if I had the answer, "What are we going to do, Jawad?"

I would tell her: "We'll just wait things out."

But we got ready for wars as if we were welcoming a visitor we knew very well, hoping to make his stay a pleasant one. During the last few weeks before the war we bought plenty of candles and canned food just in case. My mother went to Najaf to visit my brother Ammoury's grave one last time.

I remembered how we took precautions for the 1991 war and sealed the bathroom window with tape both outside and inside. They had instructed us on the TV to do so in order to protect ourselves in the event of an attack with chemical weapons. We kept plastic bottles of water in the bathroom. My mother was helping me tape the windows when I asked her what we would do if one of us needed to go to the bathroom and all three of us were already in it. She punched me on the shoulder and closed her eyes and said, "Stop it. What a disgusting thought!"

After weeks of bombing we woke up one morning to find the sky pitch black. The smoke from the torched oil wells in Kuwait had obliterated the sky. Black rain fell afterward, coloring everything with soot as if forecasting what would befall us later.

EIGHTEEN

My father used to pray in the small guest room next to the living room. The 2003 war was ten days old and I was in the throes of my perennial struggle with insomnia when I heard his footsteps going down the stairs to say his dawn prayer two minutes after the muezzin's call. Then I heard water splashing in the bathroom and figured he was performing his ritual ablutions. Minutes later the bombing started and I heard a terrible explosion that shook the entire house, nearly uprooting it. Two minutes of quiet followed, then the roar of airplanes and the sound of bombing again, but in the distance. My mother woke up and called out to my father, but he didn't answer.

"He went downstairs to pray," I shouted. I thought he was still praying and that's why he wasn't answering. But I heard no sound for another fifteen minutes, except for the calls of "God is great" echoing from the minarets. It had become a tradition to issue these calls during air raids.

I got out of bed and went downstairs. The door to the guest room was ajar, letting a bit of the candlelight into the hallway. I stood outside the room and saw him kneeling, his forehead down on the *turba*.[1] He liked to pray in the dark. When my mother once asked him why, he said that God's light was everywhere. I was thirsty so I went to the kitchen and drank some water out of the faucet. I liked

---

1. A tiny piece of the soil from the holy city of Karbala where the shrine of Hussein is. Shiites use it in their prayers.

to use the palm of my hand instead of a glass. I went back to the hallway and stood at the door of the guest room.

He was still there, kneeling, but I couldn't hear him whispering anything. He hated it when anyone interrupted his prayers. If my mother called him, he would raise his voice as he prayed to signal to her to go away and wait for him to finish. I called out his name in a hushed voice, but heard nothing. I went inside the room. I took two steps and said: "Mother is worried about you." He remained motionless. *Could he have fallen asleep in that position?* I approached and gently put my hand on his back, asking him if he was all right—but he didn't move.

I turned around to switch on the light near the door, but it didn't come on. Then I remembered that there was no electricity. I went to the hallway and brought the candle that was sitting on a plate near the edge of the stairs. I put the candle on the table and knelt next to him. I put both hands on his shoulder and called out, "What's wrong, Father?" I tried to lift him up, but he was stiff. Then his body leaned to the left and settled on its side. His eyes were shut. I rushed back to the kitchen and brought a bottle of cold water from the fridge. I sprinkled a few drops on his face to wake him up, but nothing happened. I placed my ear to his chest. His heart was still.

I heard my mother's footsteps rushing down the stairs. She yelled: "Where is Hajji?" She had a candle in her hand. She stood frozen at the door when she saw me on my knees next to him. I was calling out to him, but he was in that eternal prostration, like a fetus crouched in his mother's womb. The candle fell from her hand and she started to strike herself and scream "Oh God." She realized that his weak heart had given out after such a long journey and that he would never wake up again. She fell on her knees next to him, wailing. She took his face in her hands calling out to him as if he could still hear her. Then she started to kiss his forehead and hands, repeating "Please don't go, Hajji! Don't leave me alone. Please don't go, Hajji. Ohhh, God."

I was sad and overwhelmed by the realization that I didn't really know my father very well. I had always lied when asked about his profession, claiming that he ran a store. Was I ashamed or embarrassed? My mother kept repeating after his death that God loved him so much that he took him away while he was drawing close to him in prayer. He had undertaken the pilgrimage to Mecca three years earlier to make sure he would be with his son Ammoury in paradise. He wanted to be buried next to him in Najaf.

When I had informed him of my decision to go on studying art and that I did not want to follow him in his profession, he said, "Who will wash me then?" My mother insisted that I should be the one to wash his body. She thought it would provide the reconciliation that should have taken place when he was still alive.

"His soul will be in peace if you wash him," she said. "Please do it. For God's sake and mine."

But I refused adamantly to do so. How could I tell her that I wasn't totally convinced that there was such a thing as a soul? I had feelings of guilt because I had let him down by abandoning our ancestors' profession and had failed in my own endeavors. His assistant Hammoudy washed him. Hammoudy was like his third son and cried like a child the next morning when I told him of Father's death.

After obtaining the death certificate from the Office of Forensic Medicine, we took his body to the washhouse. Baghdad looked sad. Its streets were barren. Hammoudy had the keys to the place. We opened the door and put the body on the washing bench, but I told him I was going to wait outside. I asked him to call me should he need anything. He was surprised and asked me, "Don't you want to stay?"

I shook my head: "I can't."

The washhouse was dark, like a huge grave, except for a faint ray of light filtering in from the tiny window. I went out to the garden and squatted in front of my father's beloved pomegranate tree. It had drunk the water of death for decades, and now it was about to drink the water flowing off his body through the runnel around the washing bench. My father and I were strangers, but I had never realized it until now.

The deep red pomegranate blossoms were beginning to breathe.

When I was young, I ate the fruit of this tree that my father would pluck and bring home. But I stopped eating it when I realized that it had drunk of the waters of death. I heard the sound of water being poured inside. Seconds later I saw it rush through the runnel and flow around the roots of the tree.

I had heard on the radio the night before that the Americans were close to Najaf. I thought about the difficulties and dangers that we would encounter on our way there to bury my father.

After about forty minutes, Hammoudy called to me and I went back inside. I smelled the camphor he was sprinkling all over the shroud that covered my father's body, leaving only his face exposed. Hammoudy asked me to carry Father's body to the coffin which he had prepared and placed on the floor three meters away. He went over to the cupboard and brought out one of those special shrouds which had supplications written on it and placed it over my father's chest, tucking it right under his chin. Then he went out to the garden and I heard branches being broken. He came back with a branch of pomegranate, which he snapped in two, placing both pieces along the arms inside the coffin.

I remembered asking my father why branches of palm trees or pomegranates were placed next to the dead. He said that they lessen the pain of the grave and recited, *"In both gardens are fruit, palm trees, and pomegranates."*

Father's relatives were not able to accompany the coffin. Tradition dictated that the dead must be buried as soon as possible. The war and the bombing made it difficult to inform his relatives since all the phones were dead. Even if they had been informed, the car trip on the road to Najaf was very risky—and provided an acceptable excuse that would save them from reproach. Only a mad person would want to be inside a moving car while bombers and fighter jets were hovering overhead, ready to spit fire at any moving object. Thus it was that the only people to accompany Father on his final journey were Hammoudy, who drove his brother's car, Abu Layth, our neighbor and a longstanding friend of my father's who insisted on coming, and myself.

We carried the coffin to the car, put it on the rack on top, and secured it with ropes. The trip to Najaf usually took two hours. Baghdad's streets were empty that morning except for a few cars rushing to escape the city. Columns of black smoke billowed through the sky. I sat in the back. Nothing was said. The radio was crackling with patriotic songs and the news reported incessant bombings and battles around al-Basra and al-Nasiriyya. The Americans had reached the outskirts of Najaf, but the military spokesman stressed that our valiant soldiers and the heroes of the Fida'iyyin Saddam militias were inflicting heavy losses on the enemy and that "victory was surely ours in this final battle." And that "the enemy would be defeated at Baghdad's walls." Abu Layth made the sarcastic observation: "We keep racking up victories and keep falling behind."

The road was deserted except for the odd speeding car on the opposite side on its way to Baghdad. We were stopped near Hilla by a group of armed men wearing civilian clothes who looked like they were Fida'iyyin Saddam. One of them approached Hammoudy and asked him where we were heading. When Hammoudy told him that we had a coffin we were taking to Najaf, he said, "You won't be able to make it there. The road is very dangerous."

Hammoudy said: "But we have to bury him in Najaf."

The man replied: "Whatever. God be with you." He tapped the roof of the car with his hand.

Half an hour outside of Najaf, we saw an American platoon heading our way. Hammoudy slowed down the car and moved to the shoulder of the highway. Abu Layth advised him to stop the car, so he turned off the engine, saying, "God help us."

The platoon stopped—except for one Humvee which kept approaching. When it was about a hundred meters away it slowed down. The soldier standing on top of it pointed the gun toward us. Somewhat fearful, Hammoudy asked, "What are we going to do?"

"If we move, they will shoot us. Let's just stay still and do nothing," I told him.

The Humvee continued to approach, looking like a mythical animal intent on devouring us. Silence fell, but we could hear the whoosh of fighter jets in the distance. When the Humvee was about thirty or forty meters away, it stopped. The soldier on top shouted a number of times in English, "Get out of the car now!"

"What is he saying?" asked Hammoudy.

"He wants us to get out of the car," I said.

We opened the doors and got out of the car slowly. We left the doors open. Abu Layth and I stood to the right of the car, and Hammoudy circled around and stood in front of us.

The soldier shouted, "Put your hands up! Now! Put your hands up, now!"

I put them up and told Hammoudy and Abu Layth to do so as well. The soldier shouted again, gesturing for us to move away from the car. "Step away from the vehicle!"

Abu Layth understood and said, "Away from the car."

We moved farther away with our hands still up. Three soldiers got out of the Humvee and ran toward us screaming and pointing downward with their hands. "Down. Down. Get down on the ground."

We got down on our knees. Two of them headed toward us, pointing their guns at our heads, and stopped about five meters away. The third one circled around the car to check it out. One of them pointed to the coffin and shouted: "What's on the car?"

Hammoudy answered him, "Dead man, for Najaf."

My answer overlapped with Hammoudy's, so I repeated: "My father. Dead. Dead man."

The third soldier removed the cover of the coffin with the barrel of his machine gun and got up on the driver's side to take a look and then said, "It's a fucking coffin. Clear. Clear." He got down and circled the car, looking under it, and then came behind us. One of the two soldiers standing in front of us screamed "Don't move!" The third soldier searched us one by one with the two machine guns still pointed at us. After he finished searching Hammoudy, he dangled the car keys in front of him and jangled them, then pointed to the trunk, screaming, "You! Open the trunk."

When I translated for Hammoudy, one of the two soldiers yelled at me, "Shut the fuck up."

Hammoudy got up slowly and went back to the trunk and opened it while the third soldier followed him with the gun. He ordered him to go back where he had been so he did and got back down on his knees.

The third soldier searched the trunk. He didn't find anything and screamed "All clear! Let's get the fuck out of here."

The Humvee approached and got out of the highway and stopped in front of our car. The barrel on top of it was still pointed at us. The third soldier got back inside the Humvee. The other two retreated, but kept their gun barrels pointed at us. The Humvee stayed there. The vehicles in the battalion began to drive by fast. After the last vehicle in the convoy drove by, the Humvee that had kept watch moved away and joined the rear, leaving a storm of dust behind.

We stood up and shook off the dirt from our clothes. I realized that we'd just survived death. A slight move in the wrong direction would have resulted in a shower of bullets.

Hammoudy said, "Man, we could've all died. God saved us."

Abu Layth agreed and teased me, saying, "Wow. Your English is fluent. You should work with them as a translator."

"Nah, it's just a few sentences I learned from films and TV shows," I said.

As we got our car back on the road, Hammoudy said, "Looks like these liberators want to humiliate us."

After that incident we encountered no more trouble. An hour later, we unloaded my father's body at the cemetery and buried him next to his favorite son, Ammoury. The gravedigger approached the hole which had been dug and said in a loud voice, "O God, make this one of paradise's gardens and not a pit of fire." When he was down in the grave he said, "In the name of God, by his power and for his sake, and according to the traditions of his messenger. O God, believing in you and your book. This is what God and his messenger promised us. Verily they have told the truth. God grant us more faith and peace."

We helped one another carry my father. The gravedigger took him and laid him in the grave on his right side so that he would be facing Mecca. Then he untied the shroud and placed my father's cheek on a pillow of dirt and said: "O God. Your worshiper, the son of your worshipers, is now your guest and you are a most worthy host. God make his grave spacious, teach him his proof, join him with his prophet and protect him from the evil of Munkar and Nukayr." Then he put his hands under my father's shoulders and shook him saying: "Kazim, son of Hasan. God is your lord. Muhammad is your prophet. Islam is your religion. Ali is your imam and guardian." Then he recited the names of the twelve imams—"all righteous imams of guidance"—whereupon he began to throw dirt on him until little by little he disappeared.

Hammoudy broke down crying and covered his eyes with his hands. His tears recalled all my buried sadness and I started to cry. After a layer of dirt, the digger started to put mud on the grave. Someone said: "There is no god but God and Muhammad is his messenger. God is great. O God, your worshiper and the son of your worshipers is now your guest and you are the best host. O God, of his deeds we only know good ones, but you know him best. O God, if he was kind, be kind to him. If he has committed bad deeds, forgive him. O God, take him to your side in the uppermost chambers and let him follow his people who have long since departed this world. Bestow your mercy on him, O most merciful one. God is great. O God, be merciful to him in his estrangement, accompany him in his loneliness and calm his fears and bestow such mercy of yours so that he need not any other's. Unite him with his loved ones."

Then we started to sprinkle dirt on him and repeated with the man who led the prayer, "We are God's and to him we return."

Hammoudy hugged me and offered his condolences.

I told him, "You were like a son to him."

Then Abu Layth hugged us both and said, "He is in peace now. He was truly a good man."

We had to spend the night in Najaf. The next day we were told to fly a white flag on the car and so we did. As we approached Baghdad from the south, we passed by what resembled a graveyard of burning and destroyed vehicles and tanks near al-Rashid Military Base. There were people digging makeshift graves and burying the abandoned corpses.

NINETEEN

After Baghdad fell and the Americans occupied it there was mayhem for days. There was no electricity so we couldn't see anything on TV. It crouched there with a blind screen unable to show what was taking place. But the news on the radio spoke of mobs looting public property, ministries, the national library, and the national museum. It also said that Saddam had vanished. A few weeks before the war, the regime had released thousands of thieves and criminals from prison, but I was surprised that the Americans made no effort to protect public institutions since even occupiers were required to do so by international conventions.

I went out to get some fresh air and saw Abu Layth. We exchanged greetings, then he asked me: "Didn't you study at the Academy of Fine Arts?"

"Yeah. Why?"

"The Americans bombed it."

"The academy? Are you serious? What's the deal?"

"I don't know. That's what I heard."

It was strange to learn that the academy had become a strategic target. I decided to go and check it out myself. I put on my clothes in a hurry. My mother tried to persuade me to stay home. Although the past few days had been quiet, she was still afraid of the dangers. I told her I absolutely had to go and would be back in a couple of hours. She asked me to be very careful and saw me off with supplications for my safety.

I got into a Kia bus to Bab al-Mu'azzam, walking distance from the academy. There were mounds of garbage in the streets and an awful stench. Traffic lights were not working and drivers negotiated with signals and gestures, but there wasn't a lot of traffic. When we approached the Sarrafiyya Bridge, the driver veered to the left and slowed down, as did other cars. I turned to look back. A group of American armored vehicles were speeding toward the bridge to cross to the other side of Baghdad. The soldier standing on top of the last one had sunglasses on and pointed his gun toward us, ready to fire.

The driver was visibly annoyed by the scene and said, "What's all this about? Take it easy, man."

An old man sitting behind me proclaimed loudly, "The student is gone and the teacher is here. The student is gone and the teacher is here."

I didn't fully appreciate this sentence then, but its genius became more apparent as time passed and tragedies piled up on our chests. I found myself repeating it whenever we were slapped silly by an event.

Saddam's mural at Bab al-Mu'azzam was smeared with paint. His features had all disappeared except for part of his moustache and half of his smile. I wondered where he was, but did it even matter anymore?

Even though I had graduated many years ago, I kept visiting the academy to meet Reem throughout her graduate studies and visited her later when she became a lecturer. Even after Reem's sudden departure to Jordan, I still went there to see Professor al-Janabi. When I approached the academy that morning, I saw that part of the wall of the department of audiovisual arts had been destroyed. *So it's true!* I crossed the street and approached the main gate. The administration building had not been hit. I saw Abu Samir, the doorman, sitting on the bench and smoking as usual. I greeted him and reminded him of my name. I asked about the audiovisual building. He said: "The Americans hit it with a missile."

"When?"

"Al-Sahhaf came here to broadcast a live speech from the studio. An hour later the building was bombed."

"And nothing happened to the other buildings?"

"No, but they torched the library and all the air conditioners were stolen."

"Who stole them, who torched the library?"

"I really don't know, son. No one does. I couldn't be here when the bombing was going on. It was very dangerous. But when I returned, I saw they were gone. The rooms had locks and the locks were not broken. So those who stole them knew. Thank God some of the students came back to clean away the rubble and put things back together."

"Are any of the professors here?"

"No, none are here today."

"Excuse me. I'd like to go inside and see."

"Sure, sure. Go ahead."

I walked to the library. The iron door had been unhinged and lay a few meters away. There were pieces of rubble and metal scattered around it. I stood at the entrance and a strange smell assaulted my nose. The desk that the librarian usually sat behind was still in its place, but her chair was gone. Most of the rectangular blocks of the thick stained glass wall were hollowed out by the heat of the fire. Some of the blocks had melted and changed shape. The ceiling was covered with soot. I took two steps inside and went to the left where the book stacks used to stand. I felt a pang in my ribs when I saw heaps of ash everywhere.

I remembered the hours I had spent reading and leafing through glossy art books here. This is where I had been captured by the works of Degas, Renoir, Rembrandt, Kandinsky, Miró, Modigliani, and Chagall, de Kooning, Bacon, Monet, and Picasso. This is where I spent hours poring over images of statues by Rodin and Giacometti, my beloved Giacometti.

I stood there for ten minutes, letting my eyes wander, then walked toward the audiovisual arts department. I passed by the bench where Reem and I had sat many times. Two students were perched on it. I greeted them in passing. I saw the face of Picasso, which occupied the wall of the department of plastic arts to the right. His features looked sterner that day.

The front wall of the audiovisual department had collapsed in its entirety. The rubble was piled in front of the building, blocking the first floor. I climbed through the debris. When I got to a point high enough to see into the building, it looked like a corpse that had been skinned and then had its entrails burnt and its ribs exposed. The studio was charred and both the ceiling and floor had collapsed. The hall next door had scores of burned film reels scattered across its floor. I jumped over and went to the left. I could see the projection room. Its floor was charred and parts of the collapsed ceiling and shards of glass glittered in the sunlight. The empty seats and walls, which had witnessed so much before, were now blinded by blackness.

I climbed back over the mound of rubble and felt the wreckage I'd been carrying inside me mount even higher, suffocating my heart. I passed by the department of plastic arts. Its building was intact except for the windows. The glass had been shattered and the air conditioners removed from their metal racks. Before leaving I said goodbye to the doorman and asked him to tell Professor al-Janabi that I'd asked after him.

TWENTY

I'm standing next to a washing bench. It isn't in the *mghaysil*, but rather in some other place I've never visited. There are high ceilings, but no windows. There are neon lights, some of which blink. The bench is very long. It extends for tens of meters and has a white conveyor belt. Bodies are stacked on it. The belt moves toward the right and leads to a huge opening, and outside men wearing blue overalls and white gloves carry the bodies and throw them into a huge truck. Scores of water faucets protrude from the wall, each with an empty washbasin and a bowl under it. I hear a voice yell: "What are you waiting for?"

I turn to look for the voice and see Father sitting on a chair in the corner, his worry beads in his hand. Again the question: "What are you waiting for?" But now it comes from a different direction. I turn and see Father in another corner. I rush to the closest faucet to open it, but there is no water. The same happens with all the other faucets. I look everywhere, but Father has disappeared from every corner. The corpses keep moving to the opening on the conveyer belt.

TWENTY-ONE

The beginning of the summer break after my first year at the academy had been a pivotal point in my confrontations with Father. I'd agreed that I wouldn't work with him during the school year in order to focus on my studies, but that I would be by his side during my summer breaks. But after my first year of studies, I became convinced that I should channel all my energies on art and not go back to the suffocating atmosphere of the *mghaysil*—no matter what. I'd heard from one of my colleagues about the possibility of getting work as a house painter. He said it paid well, and I figured it could help me buy my art supplies. I could even contribute a bit to expenses at home.

Father came back from work one evening soon after I had passed my final exams and said: "Come on! Haven't you had enough rest already? When are you coming to work?"

I told him that this was something I wanted to discuss with him.

He stood at the door of the living room, his worry beads in his hand. "What is going on?"

"One of my friends . . . his father is a contractor. He paints houses. He has work for me this summer and it pays well."

Father frowned. He looked down and then stared me right in the eye and said: "Why would you want to do that? You have a good job with me."

"I thought I'd just give it a try for a few days and see."

"Do you even know how to paint?"

"It doesn't take much, Father. He said he'd teach me."

Father's disappointment was visible on his face: "So that's what it comes down to? A painter? I've been waiting all these years for someone to help me out on the job and ease my burden."

"It's just for the summer. And I'll help out with expenses here at home."

He repeated the word "painter" again as if it were a disgrace.

"What's wrong with it?" I said. "It's a decent job."

"And our profession isn't decent? Not good enough for you, is it? My father, my grandfather, and his grandfather all did it. Now you're too good for us. Well, thanks ever so much."

He went into the hall on his way to the stairs. My mother had overheard our conversation and came in from the kitchen to ask what was the matter.

"Your son would rather be a painter than do what I do," he told her as he climbed the stairs.

She asked: "Is that true, Jawad?"

"Yes, it is."

"Why, son? Your father needs you to be by his side."

"What? Is it so shameful to work as a painter?"

I got out of the chair, turned the TV off, and went out for a walk. I wanted to avoid the tense atmosphere which would continue all evening if my father and I stayed in the same room. I hadn't expected him to be happy with my decision, but I didn't think he would be totally surprised. He must have known that this day was coming. It's impossible that he didn't sense that I had lost all interest in his line of work. Once when I was young I had asked whether he had ever thought of closing the *mghaysil* or selling it when the war with Iran came to an end and Ammoury would be discharged and able to practice medicine. He said he would never retire and that his work wasn't some ordinary job but rather a way to gain favor with God. He said that I would inherit the job from him just as he'd inherited it from his father, and his father from his.

My mother told me to donate my first month's salary to Father, as tradition dictated. I did so, but he pushed my hand away and said, "Give it to your mother." My mother refused to take it—so I gave her fifty dinars as a gift that day. I used to give her a good amount of my income every month and told her to spend it on herself. Our economic situation wasn't that good, but Father owned the house, so our monthly expenses were less of a burden than for others.

My mother said that she was going to save the money I was slipping her for my dowry.

I laughed and said: "Who told you I intend to marry?"

"Sooner or later you will, my son."

When my brother Ammoury came back on leave from the front line, I told him what had happened. He scolded me because I had spoken of my plans with Father without awaiting his return. He would have known how to talk to Father and convince him, he said, or at least soften his reaction to my decision. Ammoury knew well that I could no longer deal with the *mghaysil* and its corpses. I also told him that the wages I would make from painting were twice what my father would have paid me.

Ammoury told Father that there was no sense my doing something if my heart wasn't in it. As long as I was doing something decent, he added, why not painting? He reminded Father of his own words: that in washing bodies, volition is crucial. How could I wash if I possessed no desire to do so, he asked. Ammoury made him see reason, but Father never forgave me for straying from the path.

Firas, the friend I painted with, had a great sense of humor. Although the work hours were long, they passed quickly. His father was in charge of the work and coordinated between the owners of the houses and the workers. He provided the supplies, paints, instructions, and other details. Most of the houses we worked on were newly built and unfurnished. Their owners had yet to move in.

A third coworker, Salam, was a bit older than both of us, and seasoned. He was the one who mixed the paints. If it was an old house, before we started painting, we would scrape the walls with sandpaper and fill any cracks. We would start with a coat of primer and then add the second one. I enjoyed the various stages of the process, but especially seeing how beautiful and spotless the walls and ceilings were when we were done.

After my military service, I was appointed as an arts teacher in Ba'quba. The salary was barely enough to cover one week's transportation to and from work. Why was I so naïve as to nurture the illusion that I could make a living as an artist, especially during the years of the embargo? There were some artists who were selling their paintings to foreigners. The number of foreigners had dwindled, but some journalists, diplomats, and activists still visited Baghdad and frequented the Hiwar gallery, looking for artwork. Artists also sold to Iraqi expats returning for a visit. However, most preferred traditional works or natural landscapes over abstract art. And so I began to feel bored and bitter in the late 1990s, especially as we were painting the houses of the nouveaux riches who had acquired obscene amounts of wealth by exploiting the embargo.

When I started painting houses, I'd thought that I'd only use those thick-bristled brushes temporarily before returning to the fine and feathery ones with which I felt more intimacy. But instead of the blank canvases that I could color any way I wanted and on which I could spread my imaginative visions, I found myself, for years on end, reduced to using no more than two or three colors. Pale colors on cold and monotonous surfaces. Surfaces without details or surprises, except for the odd electric switch panel or the occasional hook for a chandelier. At times a stupid fly would buzz into the sticky surface of paint and struggle there for a few seconds before dying.

TWENTY-TWO

Father rarely mentioned my uncle Sabri, who was eight years his junior. The few times the topic of Communists and their clashes with Ba'thists came up, he would say: "Sabri's people." Uncle Sabri used to visit us every now and then when I was a kid and would sleep on the floor of the guest room. He was a jovial man who always filled my pockets with sweets and played soccer with Ammoury and me in the street in front of our house. He was obsessed with the al-Zawra' team and he told me that I, too, would one day become a Zawra' fan. He was right.

The first time I attended a soccer match was with him. I was only eight years old. We went to the opening game of the national league season. I don't remember why Ammoury didn't come with us that day. It was scorching hot and there were throngs of people when we got out of the car at the Sha'b stadium. After standing in a long line, my uncle bought two pink-colored tickets for the south of the stadium. Then we stood in another line with lots of pushing and shoving to get inside. A man standing at the gate tore the two tickets in half. We made our way in and climbed to our seats in the bleachers.

The seats were beginning to fill up with fans. Some of them sang and others were beating drums. Uncle Sabri chose a spot high up, next to a group of fans carrying the white flags of Zawra'. From that spot, the field looked like a beautiful green rectangle. My uncle spread newspapers on the concrete seats and we sat down and waited for the game to start.

When the al-Zawra' players emerged from the underground

locker rooms wearing their traditional white jerseys, everyone got up. The stadium filled with applause and cheers. Uncle Sabri lifted me high so I could see. The entire team stood in the middle circle, and the players raised their arms to salute the fans on the opposite side. Chants rose. When they turned around and faced us, the applause grew even stronger. They took the field, warming up, passing balls to each another or taking shots on goal. I saw a group of photographers surrounding a bald player wearing the number eight. I asked my uncle about him. "That's Falah Hasan, the fox of Iraqi soccer," he said.

Suddenly I heard everyone around us booing and someone yelled: "Tayaran are sacks." I figured that they were heckling the opponent, Tayaran, who wore blue. But I couldn't understand "sacks." My uncle explained: "It means we will score so often they will be like sacks full of goals." My uncle put his hand on my head and stroked my hair saying: "You are a diehard Zawra' fan already."

After a scoreless first half, Falah Hasan scored with a header in the first few minutes of the second. My uncle was ecstatic and lifted me again so I could see the players hugging one another. But our joy was short-lived, because Tayaran equalized with a penalty kick. The game ended in a draw, and my uncle called the referee blind: the Tayaran striker had faked being fouled to win the penalty kick, he said. The fans chanted "Zawra', Zawra'" as we left the stadium. We walked to al-Andalus Square to catch a bus back to Kazimiyya.

I was still excited after the match and told my parents all about it and about the stadium. Father got fed up and said "Enough! You are giving me a headache with your Zawra'. God!"

My uncle took me to Zawra' games many times, and once he took me to Madinat al-Al'ab park. He and Father loved each other, but sometimes they would argue passionately about things I couldn't understand. I was ten when he visited us the last time. He would always hug and kiss me upon arrival and departure. But that time I glimpsed a sadness and clouds in his eyes when he kissed me goodbye, saying: "Don't forget your uncle."

"No, I won't forget you, but don't you forget me," I responded.

He laughed and kissed me again on my forehead. He hugged everyone tightly, especially Father.

Afterward, I asked Father about my uncle. He said that Sabri had gone to Beirut. I missed him and asked often when he would return. My mother would say, "He can't. He's busy there." I would ask about his work and when he would be finished. She never gave a straight answer, sometimes saying, "Ask your father." But Father evaded my questions too. Months later, while doing my homework, I heard on the nightly news that a number of Communist officers in the army had been executed. I heard Father tell my mother, "That's the fate of Sabri's people. They won't leave any of them alive. Thank God he escaped." I understood then that Uncle Sabri was a Communist. I asked Father, "What does it mean, being a Communist?"

"None of your business, son."

"Uncle Sabri's a Communist?"

He shushed me. "Stop asking questions. I told you it's none of your business."

When my brother Ammoury came back home, I asked him about Uncle Sabri and what communism meant. He said the Communists and Ba'thists were sworn enemies and Uncle Sabri had fled because the regime was arresting Communists. Two years later, when I was in middle school, we were all given papers to fill out to join the Ba'th Party. There were questions about relatives living abroad, and a separate sheet on which to list the names of relatives who belonged to the Communist Party or the Da'wah Party. I wrote in my uncle's full name: Sabri Hasan Jasim—Communist.

We would receive letters from him once every year or two. He would always include a line for me alone, like "kisses to my handsome Jawad. Is he still a loyal Zawra' fan cheering on my behalf?" I wrote a letter of my own to him, and we included it in the family letter. I wrote about school and Zawra's performance in the league and its new star players. I told him that I missed him very much and was waiting for him to come back.

He once called us on the phone to let us know that he was all right. Father was summoned to the directorate of secret police and was interrogated for three hours because of that one call. He wrote to my uncle after that asking him never to call again. I used to think of Uncle Sabri a lot, especially when I heard the news about the civil war in Lebanon. After his letters from Beirut, we received two from Cyprus. Then we heard that he'd gone to Aden, and we received letters with Yemeni stamps on them. He had started working as a teacher there. A civil war erupted there as well, and he had to go to Germany, where he was given asylum. He would send us money from time to time, especially in the late 1990s, when the embargo suffocated us.

After my father's death I sent a letter to Uncle Sabri in Berlin, at the last address we had for him. I told him that phone lines were all down after the bombing and we had no idea when they would be repaired. One day three months later, my mother was fluttering her hand fan, saying: "We thought the Americans would fix the electricity. How come they've only made things worse?" The absurdity of the situation could be expressed only with equal absurdity.

There was a knock at the door, and I quipped, "Maybe that's the electricity at the door waiting for your permission to come in." She laughed for the first time in weeks. I looked out the window and saw a white-haired man with sunglasses standing at the door as a taxi idled. He had turned to the other side so I could see only his back and shoulders. I went to the door and asked, "Who is it?" "Sabri," he said. "Open the door. It's Sabri."

The years had turned his hair white, leaving only some darker ash on his sideburns and eyebrows. I yelled in disbelief: "Uncle Sabri!" He hugged me tight and laughed: "Oh my, Jawad. You're taller than I am." We both cried as we kissed each other seven or eight times. He held my face in his hands as he used to do so often two decades before and repeated my name "Jawad" as if he, too, was in disbelief. My mother came to the door and said, "I can't believe it. I can't believe my eyes."

They embraced and she thanked God for his safe arrival, but chastised him: "Why didn't you tell us you were coming, Sabri, so we would prepare something."

"Prepare what? I'm not a stranger. I came to see you."

We took his suitcase out of the car and brought it inside. He paid the taxi driver and asked him to come back eight days later at six in the morning. Then he took out another small bag from the back seat and slung it over his shoulder. We went in and my mother led him toward the guest room. He said, "What is this? Am I a guest? I want to sit where we used to."

We sat in the living room. My mother offered him food, but he asked only for some water. He took off his sunglasses and put them on the table. He took out another pair of plain glasses from his pocket and put them on. He said that he was late because he had gotten lost and couldn't find the house: "Baghdad has changed so much." He had tried to call us from Amman, but the phone was dead. He looked at the black-and-white photographs of Ammoury and my father on the wall and said, "May God have mercy on their souls."

My mother brought a tray with a jug of water and a glass. She apologized that the water might not be cold enough and complained again about the electricity. She had changed into a black dress from the nightgown she had been wearing when he arrived. He thanked her and drank the whole glass. He offered his condolences to her, and she started to cry, saying: "He left me all alone."

My uncle told her, "All alone? How can you say that? Jawad is here for you."

He asked us about Father's death. My mother rushed to narrate the story she'd told before dozens of times. When she finished, he said, "May God have mercy on his soul. He is in peace now. The most important thing is that he didn't suffer."

I asked him about his trip here and when he would return.

He asked me jokingly, "Are you already sick of me and want me to leave?"

I laughed and said, "On the contrary. I hope you stay here for good and never go back."

He said that unfortunately he couldn't stay for more than a week because he had to go back to work. I asked him about his work. He said that he had studied German for four years and had been working recently as a translator for an Arabic-language German satellite channel. He had traveled from Berlin to Frankfurt and then on to Amman, where he spent a night before taking a taxi. They had left at four in the morning so that they would enter Iraq early and be able to drive through the desert highway in daylight. Driving in the dark meant risking being robbed by the many gangs and thieves operating there.

"We entered Iraq at dawn and it was a painful sight. The man welcoming me back to my country after all these years of wandering and exile was an American soldier who told me: 'Welcome to Iraq!' Can you imagine?" He said that the soldier had written his own name, "William," in Arabic on his helmet. "I told him: This is *my* country." Uncle Sabri shook his head and said that he was against the war and had demonstrated against it like millions in Germany and all over the world, but he never thought the Americans would be so irresponsible and inept. The border checkpoint with Jordan had only three soldiers and only one Iraqi official, who was wearing slippers and stamping passports. He asked the official who decided who was allowed in and who was not, and he said the American officer decided. "I just stamp."

"There was no search. Nothing," Sabri said. "Whoever wants to enter Iraq can do so very easily. So if the border checkpoint is like that, imagine how easy it is to enter from other points. Anyone coming now from Syria, Saudi Arabia, or Iran can enter." He said that one of the Iraqi officials at the border asked him for a sum of money, and when my uncle asked why he should pay, the man answered "Why not?" The driver said just to ignore him.

I told him that bribery had become endemic during the last years of the embargo and now was part of any transaction.

He said this was a process of erasure. Dictatorship and the embargo had destroyed the country. Now we had entered the stage of total destruction to erase Iraq once and for all. He took out his passport and said that even the name of the state no longer existed. The stamp simply read, "Entry-Traybeel Border Point." As if Iraq had been wiped off the map.

My mother said that if Iraqis themselves were not protective of their own country and were looting and destroying it, what should one expect strangers to do?

He said that Iraqis didn't always loot and burn public property and that even Europeans looted and burned when there was no police or law around.

I said that Europeans don't destroy museums and national libraries.

"True," he said, "but Europeans were never subject to an embargo which starved them and took them back a hundred years. They didn't have a dictator who put his name on everything so that there was no longer any difference between public property and him."

"Didn't they have Hitler?" I said.

He said the Americans hadn't supported Hitler the way they had Saddam and that they'd helped rebuild Germany after the war with the Marshall Plan.

My mother told him that we didn't want to spend all our time on politics and its headaches and that he hadn't changed in that respect even though white hair covered his entire head. He told her that that wasn't white hair, but snow from Germany which couldn't be washed away. We all laughed.

She asked whether he was craving any particular food that he hadn't tasted in years.

"Everything you cook is lovely, but Kubba is the best," he said. They both laughed. He brought out a box of sweets he'd bought from Amman and said "Here, this is for you."

I asked whether there was anything particular he wanted to do. He said he wanted to spend most of the time with us, wanted to visit my sister and her kids, but also to roam around Baghdad a bit and visit his favorite spots and look for old friends. He asked whom he might hire to drive him for a week.

I told him that a neighbor had a taxi. I reminded him of the curfew after sunset.

I told him that he would be sleeping in my room. I carried his suitcase upstairs.

The next morning I heard him singing while he shaved:

> So unfair of you
> To be gone for so long.
> What will I tell people
> When they ask about you?
> You left my heart burning
> Reeling from your absence
> So unfair of you and so cruel.
> What will I tell people
> When they ask about you?
> How could you ever
> Let me down and betray me?
> Never think my heart will heal
> Never think the pain will go away.
> What will I tell people
> When they ask about you?

I told him that we should be singing that song, reproaching him for his long absence.

"So I'm the traitor?" he asked.

"No," I said, "you just forgot about us."

He laughed and said, "I forgive you, Jawad. Wait until I tell you what happened to me."

After breakfast I left him chatting with my mother and made a deal with Hamid, the taxi driver. His only condition was not to drive anywhere outside of Baghdad, because the roads were dangerous.

Our first stop was the book market on al-Mutanabbi Street. Hamid dropped us off there. I asked him to come back for us three hours later. My uncle pored over the titles of books. After a long conversation with one of the booksellers about what he was looking for, the seller told him he had lots of poetry and history books in his warehouse across the street. My uncle told me to wait while he and the bookseller went there.

I wandered the neighborhood alone. I loved the street. It had a lot of booksellers with a surprising wealth of great titles, all the books stacked without regard to subject or genre. A timid wind blew that morning and became more self-confident around noon. It, too, leafed through books and magazines and turned pages angrily, as if it were dissatisfied with what it read and could find nothing it liked.

Many booksellers put rocks or pieces of brick on the magazines to keep them in place. Some had laid out long boards to secure a row of books without hiding their titles. Books on Shiite theology, which were previously banned, had the lion's share. New newspapers had multiplied. It was difficult to keep up with names. The lack of any law regulating publication meant that anyone with the money and the desire could start a newspaper.

In addition to newspapers, there were back issues of foreign magazines and many new Arabic magazines with glossy covers. Seduction flowed from the eyes of the female singers and movie stars on the covers. These were a few centimeters away from equally glossy posters of turbaned clerics with stern and angry faces. My uncle returned, showing me what he had found: first editions of some of al-Jawahiri's poetry collections and one of Sa'di Yusif's, together with some Jurji Zaydan novels and Neruda's autobiography.

On our way to al-Shahbandar café we saw a young man standing in front of a set of booklets and pamphlets piled on a box on the ground. He was tall and clean-shaven, in his early thirties with curly brown hair. He wore a white shirt and gray pants. We drew closer. The pamphlets bore the logo of a Revolutionary Workers' Party, of which I hadn't heard. Some of the booklets were writings by Trotsky, Lenin, and Gramsci. My uncle greeted him and started asking him about the party's links to the Communist Party.

The young man was critical of the Communist Party for many reasons, chief among them its mistaken decision to join the governing council that had been announced a few days before. That was a recognition of the occupation and a legitimization of its project. The young man spoke passionately and confidently, prefacing his sentences with "dear" or "brother," and used his right hand to illustrate main points.

My uncle told him that he himself had left the Communist Party eight years before, because he was against its practices, dubious alliances, and new trajectory. Then he asked the young man where he was from.

"Al-Thawra," he answered.

I teased him, saying "You mean al-Sadr City."[2]

"No, dear, al-Thawra City."

My uncle asked him about the popularity of Marxist ideas in al-Thawra City after all these years.

The man sounded optimistic and said that his party had active cells and good numbers there, but that the embargo had dealt a severe blow to political activism because it had destroyed the entire social fabric. "Were it not for the embargo," he said, "the regime wouldn't have survived."

My uncle was not as optimistic as this young bookseller. He asked him what he thought about the rise of sectarian discourse and how religious thinking had struck deep roots during the years of the embargo. The man responded that compared with other countries in the region, the history of secularism in Iraq was well known, and that religious parties had no solutions to offer, just obscurantism. Islamic movements had failed anyway in the Arab world, he said.

A devout man who was listening to the conversation started to argue with the young man. My uncle took this as an opportunity to leave. He took some of the booklets and gave the young man some money as a donation. The man thanked him and invited us to visit the party's temporary headquarters, in the Rafidayn Bank at the

---

2. Al-Thawra (Revolution City) is Baghdad's Shiite ghetto, where 1.5 million poor working-class families live. Its name was changed to Saddam City in the 1980s. After the 2003 war, it was renamed al-Sadr City in honor of the cleric who was opposed to Saddam and was assassinated under his rule.

beginning of Rashid Street. My uncle asked, "Are you the ones who looted the bank?"

The man laughed and said, "No, we arrived too late." My uncle joined in the young man's laughter.

After we had left, I asked what he thought of what the bookseller had said.

The young man was too optimistic, especially about secularism, Uncle Sabri said, then acknowledged that perhaps it's necessary to be optimistic. He added that he was reminded of one of his favorite quotes from Gramsci: "Pessimism of the intellect. Optimism of the will." He himself was rather pessimistic about sectarianism. What had taken place, he said, was not just an occupation but the destruction of a state more than eighty years old. War and occupation were the final blows, but the process had begun with the destruction of the infrastructure during the 1991 war. Then there was the embargo, which had destroyed the social fabric, and now the void created by the occupation was being filled by these sectarian parties because they had institutions. Their rhetoric touched people's hearts and they knew how to exploit the political climate. But, my uncle added, the history of secularism in Iraq runs deep. The Da'wa Party, for example, was founded in Najaf, because with the spread of communism even in Najaf and Karbala, people were confusing Shiite with Shiyu'i (Communist), which terrified the religious clerics.

We had reached al-Shahbandar café. I asked: "Did you see all the posters of clerics and all the theology books being sold?"

He said, "Of course, after long years of suppression there is a thirst, but perhaps it will be quenched."

We entered the café, found two empty seats, and ordered tea. There was a French TV crew conducting interviews with intellectuals. I saw the famous theater director Salah al-Qasab sitting a few meters away. They approached him, but I heard him decline more than once to be interviewed. The journalist insisted and asked him through the translator: "What do you have to say about what has happened?"

"Film the streets of Baghdad. That's what I think," he answered.

Ten minutes later my uncle saw a man with a stack of newspapers under his arm. He was handing out copies of *Tariq al-Sha'ab*, the mouthpiece of the Communist Party. They hugged and chatted for fifteen minutes and then Sabri came back with a copy. He told me that the man was an old comrade whom he'd last seen in Beirut in 1982.

I searched for a familiar face, but I didn't see any of the people I usually saw here. My uncle started reading the newspaper. There were announcements about public funerals for the party's martyrs who had been executed years ago. There was an announcement in big letters about a major demonstration in three days to commemorate the anniversary of the 14th of July revolution. It called on all the party's friends and supporters to assemble at Liberation Square to march to Firdaws Square. My uncle asked whether I was interested in taking part.

"Sure," I said. "First, to be with you and second, to go to a demonstration freely for the first time in my life, without being forced to do so. I have to do it for the sake of variety at least." We both laughed.

I looked at my watch and reminded him that it was time to meet our driver. We got out and passed by the young commie again. He greeted us from a distance and we smiled back. My uncle asked Hamid to drive him to the new headquarters of the Communist Party, which was at the insurance building at al-Andalus Square.

"I thought you said you had divorced the party?" I asked.

"Yeah, but I just want to get some news about my comrades . . . ask about some of them and see who's been back. I won't be long," he said.

I was feeling sleepy so I told him I'd take a nap in the back seat until he came back. When he returned, his smile had disappeared. I asked what was wrong. "Nothing," he said.

The next day the electricity was back on long enough to see on TV the official announcement of the formation of the governing council under the aegis of Paul Bremer. The council was a hodgepodge of names supposedly representing the spectrum of Iraqi society, but we had never heard of most of them. What they had in common was that each name was preceded by its sect: Sunni, Shia, Christian . . . We were not accustomed to such a thing. My uncle was furious when he saw the secretary general of the Iraqi Communist Party sitting with the other members. He'd heard at the headquarters that the party had polled its cadres and that they'd voted to be part of the council, but he still couldn't believe his eyes.

He waved his hand and said, "Look at him, for God's sake. They put him there as a Shiite, and not because he represents an ideological trend or a party with its own history of political struggle. What a shame that this is what it all comes down to. Now an entire history of resisting dictatorship and rejecting war is being trashed. Communists will be like all these other fuckers and crooks. Look at them. Each has a belly weighing a ton."

Nevertheless, we went to Liberation Square on the morning of July 14th. My uncle said he wanted to commemorate the revolution and the sacrifices of Communists despite what had become of the party in recent years. Hundreds had gathered under the Liberty Monument. I had not stood under it or passed by it for a long time. It was a bit dirty, because of all the pollution and negligence. It looked like it desperately needed maintenance and restoration, but it still had that aura. I remembered Mr. Ismael and my dreams of becoming a great artist—which had all now evaporated.

There were many Communists present, of course, and the organizers wore red ribbons around their arms. But many others seemed to be sympathizers, or perhaps found themselves closer to the Communist Party than to any of the other sectarian parties. There were even a few veiled women. Perhaps many were attracted by the slogan on many of the placards carried by some: "No to Occupation, Yes to Democracy." There were other banners as well, many red flags, and posters of Abdilkarim Qasim, who was the first prime minister after the pro-British monarchy was toppled in 1958. I was used to reading his name in the context of condemnations by the Ba'thists because he had supposedly been a dictator. That Saddam had participated in a failed assassination attempt on Qasim's life had been one of those heroic epics repeated to us hundreds of times, so it was quite strange for me to see Qasim's image being paraded about, not to condemn him, but in celebration of his memory.

My uncle was one of those who believed that, despite his mistakes, Qasim was the first indigenous Iraqi to rule the country in the twentieth century and that he had accomplished important feats. He said as he pointed to the American soldiers who were monitoring the spectacle from a Humvee that the Americans had been against Qasim and had helped the Ba'thists overthrow him.

The mood was festive. A group played popular music and many danced. I even saw a woman in her sixties applauding and dancing along. My uncle said that she was a veteran Communist who'd returned from exile in London. He knew her because of the articles she regularly published on leftist websites. Passing cars were honking to salute the demonstration. My uncle seemed enthusiastic despite his dismay with the party for its decision to enter the governing council.

I told him that seeing the demonstration one would think that the Communist Party could win the elections in a landslide and rule the country. When I heard some of the demonstrators chanting "Fahad, Fahad, your party isn't dead and will live forever," I asked him who this Fahad might be. He was shocked.

"Fahad was the founder of the party," he said. "He was executed by the monarchy and famously said right before being executed, 'Communism is stronger than death and higher than the gallows.' You have to read Batatu's book on Iraq. It's the most important and encyclopedic account of Iraq's modern history."

I promised that I would look for it and he said he would send me a copy if I couldn't find one. After about an hour, the crowd began to move toward Firdaws Square. The demonstration was well organized. When we were marching down Sadoun Street, Uncle Sabri kept looking back to get an idea of the numbers. When we reached Firdaws Square, the crowd had swelled. American choppers hovered over us.

Later events proved any optimism about secularism misplaced. In the weeks following that big demonstration, many other rallies were organized by other parties. They were saturated with religious and sectarian symbols. The sectarian stamp became normal and began to acquire unusual impact. In time the Communist Party's popularity dwindled, and its performance in elections was dismal; its secularism meant that it would be the last horse in the sectarian race. No one would place bets on it.

As we left the Communists' demonstration that day, my uncle surprised me by expressing his desire to go to the Martyr's Monument—the one designed by Ismail Fattah al-Turk. He said he'd seen pictures of it, and had read an article by a German critic who said that it was one of the most beautiful monuments he'd ever seen. He said he wanted to see it in its actual dimensions. From al-Andalus Square we headed in the direction of al-Sha'b Stadium. I asked whether he remembered indoctrinating me as a Zawra' fan.

"Of course I remember!" he said, laughing. He asked about the Indoor Sports Hall next door.

"That's the Saddam Indoor Hall," I said.

"What will they call it now? The Bush Hall?"

We could see the severed sky-blue dome of the monument from afar. It looked as if it were closing in on itself as we approached. He took out his camera and started to snap pictures. "It's gorgeous," he said. The Olympic Committee building was across the street from the monument. Huge sections had collapsed and all that was left was a metal skeleton. He asked me about it. I told him that that had been Uday's headquarters. He looked and took a few pictures and then turned back to the monument.

We were in front of the main gate. American soldiers were stationed at the monument and had turned it into a barracks. Concrete blocks and barbed wire barricaded the gate and soldiers with machine guns stood guard. Armored vehicles and Humvees were parked inside along the path that led to the monument itself.

I remembered how Reem and I had visited it after it was opened to the public back in 1989. Despite our objection to the war and its glorification, we were impressed by the monument's beauty. I was deeply offended and angered when I saw the American soldiers and armored vehicles occupying a place which symbolized the victims of war—victims such as my brother and thousands of others. My uncle said that it was a premeditated insult, calculated for its symbolic significance. It was not a matter of logistics.

After the Martyr's Monument he asked Hamid to take us to al-Rashid Street.

Hamid told him that most stores would be closed and he wouldn't be able to buy anything.

My uncle told him that he wasn't going there to shop. He just hadn't seen the street for more than two decades.

It was about five in the afternoon and the street was already empty. Hamid said that crime was rampant and that there were a lot of killings and robberies. Most shop owners weren't even opening their shops, and those who did closed early.

The spectacle broke my uncle's heart. "This is what al-Rashid Street has become? It was always bustling with people. Look at it now."

Two days before leaving, he told me that he was craving *masguf*.[3] I told him that my mother would be more than happy to make that wish come true if we could buy fish. He refused and said that he would take me out to a restaurant.

When I asked why, he said that he'd read that fish from the river would be tainted because all the rivers were polluted with depleted uranium and untreated sewage.

I was impressed that he'd kept up with the news about Iraq when he was in Germany. But I said that the fish at the restaurant would be from the same river.

---

3. A traditional Iraqi meal of barbequed fish from the Tigris, prepared with spices and slowly cooked over coal.

"No, they raise them in special farms."

It was a lovely dinner, because we recalled some of our memories together. I asked whether he ever got fed up or bored with reading the news.

He said that every now and then he would promise himself not to read any more news, but then would give up after a few days. It was just impossible. It was an addiction. He asked me about my plans, and I told him that my dream was to study art abroad, in Italy or somewhere else. He was supportive and said that although his means were limited, he would help me find information about scholarships and grants and would ask a friend of his who taught art in Holland for advice.

I told him that what worried me the most was leaving my mother behind, under the current political situation.

"Of course, but let's put our heads together and come up with a solution," he said.

I asked whether he was planning to visit again anytime soon.

"It's very difficult to get time off from work and, to be honest, I was very happy to see you all, especially you, but my heart was broken. I used to follow the news about Iraq day by day on the radio, newspapers, TV, and recently on the Internet. I never missed a piece of news. I knew the embargo had destroyed the country, but it's different when you see it with your own eyes. It's shocking. The entire country and every one in it are tired. I mean even right here in Karrada. Wasn't this the most beautiful neighborhood? Look at it now. Then you have all this garbage, dust, barbed wires, and tanks. There aren't any women walking down the street anymore! This is not the Baghdad I'd imagined. Not just in terms of the people. Even the poor palm trees are tired and no one takes care of them. Believe me, these Americans, with their ignorance and racism, will make people long for Saddam's days."

The week went by very quickly. On the night before Uncle Sabri's departure the family gathered to say goodbye. My sister, Shayma', her husband, Sattar, and their two kids came over. Sattar chatted with my uncle but apologized, as usual, because he was busy with work and stayed only half an hour. Shayma' said that he was working with one of the Iraqi returnees in a new construction company which was about to get many reconstruction contracts. Upon hearing that, my mother said, "Why don't they fix the electricity first?" Since there was none, we had lit candles before starting to eat dinner. My uncle joked that in Germany people would pay a lot of money to dine in such a romantic setting.

The next morning he insisted on buying us a satellite dish as a gift. He said that we had to "breathe a bit" and see all that we missed during those years of suffering under the embargo and Saddam. The technician was about to finish programming the satellite dish when the electricity was cut off again, so we agreed that I would pass by his store, which was close by, the next day when the electricity came back on. Eventually, the dish became our only window through which we could see the world and the extent of our own devastation, which multiplied day after day.

Our goodbyes that morning floated in tears as we drank our tea. My mother took Sabri to task for going everywhere around the city but not visiting his brother's and nephew's graves. He told her that he never visited graves and didn't need to see them to remember the people buried there. He put his hand on his heart and said "Ammoury and Abu Ammoury are right here in my heart."

He gave me an envelope with five hundred American dollars and insisted that I take it to help us get through until things improved. He was confident that we would see each other again in the near future. My mother cried as she hugged him and told him, "Don't disappear for another twenty-five years!" She sprinkled water behind his car to make sure he returned.

A month after his departure he sent me a long sorrowful and pessimistic article about his visit that he had published online. It was entitled "A Lover Pauses before Iraq's Ruins." Its most beautiful section dealt with palm trees:

> Iraqis and palm trees. Who resembles whom? There are millions of Iraqis and as many, or perhaps somewhat fewer, palm

trees. Some have had their fronds burned. Some have been be-headed. Some have had their backs broken by time, but are still trying to stand. Some have dried bunches of dates. Some have been uprooted, mutilated and exiled from their orchards. Some have allowed invaders to lean on their trunk. Some are combing the winds with their fronds. Some stand in silence. Some have fallen. Some stand tall and raise their heads high despite everything in this vast orchard: Iraq. When will the orchard return to its owners? Not to those who carry axes. Not even to the attendant who assassinates palm trees, no matter what the color of his knife.

When al-Ja'fari was chosen to be the prime minister, my uncle wrote to me: "Marx used to say that 'history always repeats itself twice, the first time as tragedy, the second time as farce.' And what we are witnessing now in Iraq is a farce. Who would've ever believed that Iraq's prime minister would be from the Da'wa Party, spear-heading a backward sectarian list? When I left Iraq, the Da'wa Party was banned and later the Americans placed it on the list of terrorist organizations. Now Bush shakes hands with al-Ja'fari? It's a bizarre world."

TWENTY-THREE

Every evening, I would sit in front of the computer screen for three or four hours, oblivious to the passage of time. I was enchanted by this world—this universe—to which we had had no access during the embargo. Getting the Internet at home was still too expensive, and I didn't even have a desktop computer, but the fees at the Internet café were reasonable. I would usually start with a quick tour of local and Arab newspaper sites to read what the world was saying about our ongoing disasters. I discovered an Iraqi site called Uruk. It resembled Iraq itself in its political topography and chaos. The administrators allowed anyone and everyone to publish (or at least did not prohibit it), irrespective of their background and leanings. So I would find some profound and penetrating analysis or satire right next to offensive, sectarian, and racist thoughts and never-ending conspiracy theories. Also posted were a lot of documents exposing the new politicians and the corruption, which had gotten out of hand. After reading some of these, I would begin my daily roaming—usually quite random. I started a Hotmail account to correspond with my uncle and try to locate Reem. I was hopeful that I would somehow reconnect with her.

I was proud to learn that some of my classmates who had emigrated years ago had become quite successful. Many had their own websites showcasing their works. But I couldn't help feeling bitter and jealous when I saw that some who didn't have a fourth of my talent had established their names in Amman and other places, thanks to good PR. I started to dream of the day when I, too, would have my own website, but I remembered that first I had to start producing art again.

TWENTY-FOUR

He knocked at the door about a month after Father had passed away. He was in his late forties and short. His gray beard was neatly trimmed and edged with white. He wore round glasses with a silver frame. The bridge of his big nose left a space between his honey-colored eyes. The eyes sat under thick salt-and-pepper eyebrows. He was wearing a flowing black robe and a white turban. After greeting me, he extended his hand and offered his condolences. "May you have a long life, son. I am Sayyid Jamal al-Fartusi. Forgive me, but I heard only yesterday." I thanked him and invited him in. He told a young man who was driving his car to wait for him. I opened the door to the guest room and showed him in. I gave him a seat and asked my mother to make coffee.

He said he'd known my father for years and had wanted to be at the funeral, but the war and the Americans had prevented him from doing so. A few minutes later my mother knocked at the door. I got up to open it and took the tray from her. I offered him the coffee. He took the cup and the saucer and put it on the table to the right of the chair. After a few sips he asked me about the circumstances of my father's death. I told him Father had died in the very room we were sitting in while kneeling in prayer. He was moved and repeated twice, "May God be exalted." Then he said, "May he welcome him in his vast paradise."

After a heavy silence, he asked me: "Did you work with your father?"

"No."

"How come? My son, the one you just saw waiting outside in the car, works with me and his two brothers as well."

"God didn't will it."

He smiled. I asked him how he came to know my father. He said that for ten years he'd been in charge of collecting unclaimed, abandoned, and unidentified corpses from hospitals and from the morgue. He saw to it that they were washed, shrouded, and properly buried.

"Is it a governmental department or a charity?" I asked.

"No, it's unofficial. Just a personal initiative I started myself, but I have an agreement with the Ministry of Health and Hospitals. This is how I came to know your father, God have mercy on his soul. He washed some of the bodies we found."

"And how are things nowadays?"

"It's very chaotic. I'm sure you know that most ministries were looted and destroyed, but the Ministry of Health wasn't, as far as I know. I'm waiting for things to settle down, so I can continue. I'm trying to get permissions from the American army so they don't attack my trucks and team when they go around the city. But even the Americans are disorganized. Each one sends me somewhere else. First they said I had to go to the Green Zone—you know, where the palace used to be—but then they wouldn't let me go in. They said I had to get permission and forms from the Conference Center, but nothing materialized."

"And who covers the expenses?"

"There are still a lot of good human beings in this world. I receive monthly donations."

"God bless you and may there be more like you."

"Well, why don't you work with us then, like your father did? I'm sure you know how to wash."

"Yes. I learned it from him and worked with him for a while, but that was years and years ago. Hammoudy, who used to work with my father, has taken over the place and will be working there. You can discuss it with him."

"Oh, that's great. I know Hammoudy."

Hammoudy had approached me a week after my father died about taking over the *mghaysil*. He suggested paying us half of the income as rent. I agreed without much thought, because we desperately needed the money. The housepainting market was dead, and I was looking hard for any type of work, without success. Instead of Iraq becoming a new Hong Kong, as the Americans had promised, there was chaos and massive unemployment. I said goodbye to the man, never imagining that he would come back into my life.

TWENTY-FIVE

"So you think painting or making statues is better than my honorable and rewarding profession?"

Father had often wounded me with this question when I told him of my desire to become a sculptor. I was burning to tell him now. They are stealing statues these days, Father. They stole Abdilmuhsin al-Sa'doun's statue, melted it, and sold it. Those who don't steal statues pull them down because they want to rewrite history. Ironically, they are imitating their sworn enemy, who himself tried to rewrite history from a Ba'thist perspective, destroying many statues and putting up new ones in their place.

History is a struggle of statues and monuments, Father. I will not have a share in all of this, because I have yet to sculpt anything important. Even Saddam's huge statue in Firdaws Square was brought down right after your death. I thought I would be happy since I detested him so much, but I felt I'd been robbed of the happiness. That was not the end I had imagined. Those who brought him down were the ones who put him there in the first place. They armed him to the teeth in the war that killed Ammoury, your favorite son. Now some want to sever the head of Abu Ja'far al-Mansour, the founder of Baghdad, and bring down the statue of the poet al-Mutanabbi. Even the statues are too terrified to sleep at night lest they wake up as ruins.

TWENTY-SIX

I thought I had succeeded in distancing myself from death and its rituals during the two years following Father's death. But I discovered that even though I wasn't dealing directly with it with my own hands, death's fingers were crawling everywhere around me. I couldn't shake the notion that death was providing my sustenance. For a time I leaned on a rationalization: *What has really changed? Weren't things the same when my father was the provider? Didn't I eat and drink what death earned for us, one way or another? I used to contribute a bit to the household expenses. The only difference now is that death is more generous, thanks to the Americans.*

Hammoudy stopped by at the end of every month to give me half of the earnings. Whenever I asked him how things were at the *mghaysil*, he said that there were more and more corpses. I knew that already, because the amount he gave me was increasing month by month. I asked about the men he washed. He said most had been killed by the Americans, but there were also many victims of the unprecedented wave of crime, as well as those blown up by car bombs and other explosions.

All my attempts to find a job failed. I started to spend most of my time reading and browsing the Internet. Ufuq café on al-Zahra Street near our house became a daily stop for me. I was naïve when I chose "giacometti" for a username for my e-mail account. Hundreds of others had chosen it too. After several variations were rejected, I settled for his name together with the year I was born. I looked for Reem the first few days, but to no avail. I had been seriously thinking of continuing to study sculpture abroad. I realized that getting a scholarship was not easy and that not only would it be expensive to travel and live abroad, but it would be almost impossible to transcend the language barrier. My English amounted to the little I had learned at school and a few sentences I had picked up from films. Nevertheless, I started to gather information and wrote to a few institutes and arts colleges. Their answers were usually formulaic: they thanked me for my interest, advised me to read the prerequisites and requirements, and stressed the issue of the visa.

I asked Professor al-Janabi for advice. He was encouraging and promised to write a letter of recommendation, but reminded me of the importance of having a strong portfolio to increase my chances of acceptance. I had not participated in any exhibitions since graduation. He told me straight up that I had to get serious again about producing art. I bought a small digital camera to take photographs of some of my old works.

Three months after the invasion, Professor al-Janabi called me on my new cell phone. He said that the French Cultural Center was organizing an exhibition of young and marginalized artists and encouraged me to participate. I could submit only one work, so I chose one that had caused some trouble back when I was still studying. It was a strange-looking iron chair I had found thrown out on the street while wandering around with Reem near the academy. It was old and had some rust on it. I decided to carry it off. Reem laughed coquettishly: "Are you already furnishing the nest?" "You know I'm against the idea of marriage," I said. "I just got an idea for a piece." When I took it to the academy to put it in our shop, the security guard ridiculed me, saying, "What's this? Are you selling scrap now?"

I bought some metal chains from Bab al-Agha and added them to the chair's arms and front legs to make it look like a torture chair. I had planned on submitting the work to the annual exhibition, but Reem said I would be endangering myself for no reason. Professor al-Janabi agreed that it was too dangerous. I even thought about adding a tiny cage to it and putting a real bird inside. Reem said it was a good idea, but she preferred it with the chains alone and no cage or bird. "It doesn't change the main idea and it's still dangerous to show it." Al-Janabi liked it a lot, so I gave it to him as a gift. He refused at first, but I told him it would be an honor if he accepted. The chair stayed in his office all those years. He made sure not to put anything on it despite the piles of papers and books he had in his office. He gladly lent it back to me for the exhibition, and it was accepted.

I stopped by his office to take the chair home, intending to clean it up a bit and add some red dye to resemble drops of blood. The professor seemed anxious. He said that there were rumors about revenge against anyone who had been a member of the Ba'th Party. I laughed, saying that it was obvious he wasn't a real Ba'thist, that, like so many, he had been forced to join, in his case to gain approval for his scholarship to Italy. He said people were trying to settle scores. "Let's hope for the best."

We were told to bring our works two days before the opening. I took a taxi to the French Cultural Center at Abu Nuwas Street. The streets were crowded and chaotic, full of bumps and craters because of the bombing. I was afraid at first that the chair, which I had put in the trunk, would be damaged, but then I remembered that it was made of iron.

Only one of the two lanes was open to traffic. Cars were driving in both directions in the same lane. The eastern side of the street had huge American tanks parked on it. When we approached al-Firdaws Square, where the big hotels are, American soldiers had blocked the streets and were motioning to everyone to turn around and go back. The driver sighed and made a U-turn. We took al-Sadoun Street to al-Karrada and arrived at the building. I had passed by it many times years before when Reem was taking French classes there. It had a nice café in the back garden where we would some-times sit. The last time I was here was the day she finished her French course. Her classmates had gathered in the courtyard to take pictures. Fifteen minutes later a GMC truck with tinted windows parked on the sidewalk right under the "No Parking" sign. The driver turned the flasher on and a man wearing khaki came out of the passenger side. He approached the group which had been exchanging good wishes and congratulations and asked who had used the camera—"Photography is not allowed here." He snatched the camera from one of the female students, took the film out and warned everyone not to do it again. He went outside, got into the car and took off. Most of us were surprised, but we later realized that the presidential palace was just across the river. Now the Americans have occupied it and surrounded it with walls and checkpoints; our new rulers can live far away from us.

Finally arriving at the center, I asked the organizers to put my piece in a dark corner away from windows, but close to where I could still plug in the projector light I had added to it to make it look like an interrogation or torture chair. The opening ceremony was held in the afternoon, because having it at night would be too dangerous and would violate the curfew. Nevertheless, the ceremony was uplifting. It included a short speech by the French cultural attaché, then another by one of the academy's professors, full of hope for a future filled with freedom. Many of us were hopeful in those days that there would at least be some sort of new beginning for people to start a better life despite all the destruction. The occupation would come to an end sooner or later. I was surprised that some of the participating artists went overboard in praising the Americans, as if they'd actually come here for our sake. I was happy to see Sergio de Mello, the United Nations representative in Iraq, at the exhibition. He and the three men accompanying him paused before each work. He paused much longer before mine, saying through his interpreter: "Very powerful." Then he shook my hand and covered it with his left and thanked me twice.

The participants in the exhibition included those who had graduated a few years earlier, but who refused, for political and ethical reasons, to have their work co-opted by the politics of the time. The exhibition went on for a week, and the responses were positive. A film crew that was working on a documentary about dictatorship and occupation conducted interviews with many of us. One of them was an Iraqi based in New York who spoke with me about my piece. I asked him to send me the interview on a tape or CD and he promised to do so, but I never received anything. I never knew whether he just forgot, or whether the package had been stolen. Their film was shown a year later on the al-Arabiyya channel. I waited for even a few seconds of the interview or a glimpse of the exhibition, but there was nothing. What they did show were images of the destruction at the academy and of all the bombing and looting. There were also interviews with some poets at al-Mutanabbi Street. I was suspicious of all the Iraqis who had come back after many years abroad. Many of them either came with the tanks and the militias or returned to make money or get a hot story and then forget all about us.

A month after the exhibition, I saw men on TV looking for de Mello's corpse in the rubble of the Qanat Hotel. I was heartbroken. A huge truck full of explosives had blown up the hotel which served as the UN's headquarters in Baghdad. De Mello and many others were killed. A few days later, Muhammad Baqir al-Hakim was assassinated in Najaf. Explosions multiplied. They went after important personalities at first, then targeted average folk who had nothing to do with what was taking place but whose lives became a currency that was easy to circulate and liquidate. We'd thought the value of human life had reached rock-bottom under the dictatorship and that it would now rebound, but the opposite happened. Corpses piled up like goals scored by death on behalf of rabid teams in a never-ending game. That is the thought that came to mind when I heard "Another car bomb targeted . . . "

Following each round, human remains were plucked from a mixture of blood and dirt. The ones who remained in one piece without losing an eye or their entire head were fortunate. The American referee had killed enough already and now was killing only sporadically, allowing the local players, who were even more ferocious, to carry on. But even those who picked up the pieces and cleaned up what death left on the city's face were not safe from death.

TWENTY-SEVEN

Hammoudy went to the Shorja market one Thursday at the end of August. He was rapidly running out of camphor and ground lotus leaves for the *mghaysil*. He had told me that he now needed to restock once a month instead of every six months as he used to do before the war.

Hammoudy did not come back home that day, nor the following day. His cell phone was turned off and he didn't respond to the text messages that his wife and his brother, who worked at an electronics store, had sent him. There had not been any bombs or explosions at the Shorja market that day—or even that month. For two days they looked for him in the hospitals nearby and went to police stations without coming up with anything. People told them to go to the morgue. His brother looked at all the photos they had of all the bodies piled up everywhere in that place, which couldn't cope with the numbers, but found nothing. He looked in the mounds of corpses for the green ring Hammoudy used to wear on his left hand. He still goes there from time to time, asking, just in case something turns up. Hammoudy's mother doubled her visits to al-Kazim's shrine nearby. Al-Kazim was known for fulfilling wishes and never letting down those who sought his intercession. She even pledged to walk all the way to Najaf if Hammoudy came back safe, but he has yet to return.

Did someone kidnap him thinking that he was a wealthy merchant? Neither his appearance nor his age would lead anyone to think that. Kidnappers usually call the family to demand a ransom and never deliver the body until they get their money, or some of it. No one ever called. Hammoudy never came back, even though his mother walked to Najaf three times.

TWENTY-EIGHT

Reem, too, disappeared all of a sudden, just as Hammoudy did. It was seven years ago, but unlike Hammoudy's, her kidnapper was not human or nameless. I called her at home one morning in August. The phone kept ringing. There were no cell phones back then. I called again in the evening and no one picked up. Our secret sign before was to have the phone ring once and then hang up and she would call me back. But after our engagement we could speak freely in front of her father and stepmother. She had convinced me to ask for her hand, and I overcame my hesitation. I didn't have any savings and my income wasn't even enough to rent an apartment. Having her live with us at home was out of the question. I had no desire to start a family, but she kept telling me that years were passing and she was getting tired of doing everything in secret and struggling just to be together. She persuaded her father to agree to the marriage. He had hesitated a bit at first, because of my father's profession and my financial situation, but she told him that I intended to travel abroad and do graduate studies. Her stepmother, happy to get rid of Reem once and for all, helped convince her husband to let us live in one of the houses he owned in al-Sayyidiyya after we got married.

I, too, had to get my parents' approval, especially since marrying a divorcee was frowned upon. My mother had met Reem once when I invited her and another colleague to lunch at our house. She liked her, but I didn't tell her that we had something going on. When I told her we were thinking of marriage, she asked, "Why did you choose this divorced woman out of all the others?" I told her that my heart had chosen. She agreed, but grudgingly. I asked her to try to convince Father. All he had to do was accompany me to Reem's house to formally ask her father. Father didn't mind that she had been married before. Perhaps he was moved by the fact that her ex-husband was a martyr, like his son. He asked me about her family and her father's line of work. He wasn't convinced that I was in a position to marry a woman from a rich family. In the taxi to their house he asked me terse questions about where we planned to live, the dowry, and other questions to which I had no clear answers.

The distance between our house in Kazimiyya and theirs in al-Jadiriyya was the gulf between two classes and two worlds. I thought of the problems and tensions we would be confronting because of that chasm. Father had never set foot in al-Jadiriyya. What was he thinking about when he looked through the taxi's window at those huge modern houses? Was he thinking that I was about to sever my last bond to him and that I had succeeded, at long last, in leaving his sphere?

We stood at the main gate. There were three cars parked in the long garage. To the right there was a big garden with a neatly trimmed lawn edged on all sides with flowers. A palm tree towered over the far right corner. Below it was the Arabic Jasmine from which Reem used to pluck flowers for me. I rang the bell and we both waited. Father looked up at the two-story house and the adjacent houses. I looked at my shoes to make sure they were spotless and fixed my necktie. It was the first time I'd worn a tie and jacket in years. Father didn't even own a necktie. He wore a sky-blue shirt and a dark jacket, and had put a skullcap over his head. Reem's father emerged from the wooden door and walked toward us. We shook hands. He led us back through the door to the guest room.

He was very proper, but there were invisible barriers he didn't care to cross. We exchanged pleasantries and the ritual went on as usual. He asked us what we would like to drink: juice, tea, or Arabic coffee? We both asked for coffee. He went to the door, which was ajar, and relayed our request. They had a maid, but I knew that Reem was going to bring the coffee, since that was what ritual dictated.

I knew from her footsteps that she was about to enter. She was wearing medium-heeled black shoes, which accentuated her slenderness as she walked, a black skirt just below the knees and a blue shirt with long loose sleeves. She had on her favorite silver bracelets, and her fingernails were painted creamy white. She offered the coffee to Father and invited him to take a piece of chocolate as well. He thanked her. Then she turned to me. We exchanged a smile as I took the coffee and chocolate. I couldn't resist stealing a glimpse at her cleavage. In deference to the occasion, she was not as generous that day as she usually was, so I couldn't see much. She seemed a bit timid, as if she knew what my eyes were searching for.

A heavy silence fell. My attempts to initiate a conversation that could engage both my father and hers failed. Both were laconic and kept what they said to the minimum. My father wasn't chatty to start with. Her father seemed to believe that he had been forced to seal an unprofitable deal. On the way back, Father warned me against depending too much on Reem and her father. Don't become a "burden" on them, he said. I was hurt by that word, but said nothing. The years had taught me that it was futile to argue with him.

The engagement ring gave us a freedom we had not enjoyed before. I started to visit her at home, and we could go out together for hours far more often than before. But this sweetest of times lasted only three months. Reem suddenly disappeared.

I kept calling, but there was no answer. In the evening I went to their house and rang the bell, but no one came to the door. I noticed there were only two cars, Reem's and her stepmother's. Her father's car was not there. The curtains were shut and the gate was locked. I was baffled. I went home and called her friend Suha. She said that they'd left that morning for Jordan and that she had no idea when they would be back.

I thought of all possibilities, but couldn't find a convincing explanation. If her father had forced her to leave, she would have called and asked for help. I knew he was thinking of leaving the country and had increased his business in Jordan and Turkey, but still. I went to his office in Karrada to inquire. One of his assistants said that he didn't know, but perhaps his wife was ill and had gone to Jordan for treatment. I thought that Reem must have gone along with her and would return soon. I convinced myself that she would call, send a letter, or just return and surprise me, but she never did.

A month and a half later, one of the drivers at her father's company hand-delivered a letter from her. I recognized her handwriting on the envelope. I opened it right away and read it while standing. It was written in blue ink on elegant paper:

Darling,

You will always be darling to me no matter what happens. Please forgive my absence and sudden departure and my not telling you anything. Maybe you will forgive me after reading this letter. I hope you understand me, just as you always have, with an open heart after you listen so lovingly and patiently. The last thing I want to do in the world is to hurt you, or be away from you. When I am far away from you I am far from myself. Please believe me when I say that you are more precious than anything in this world and my love is what compelled me to do what I did.

Two months ago while showering, I felt a tiny lump in my left breast. I went to the doctor, but didn't say anything to you at the time, because I didn't want you to worry. The doctor decided that they would remove it and do a biopsy. It turned out that it was malignant. My father insisted that we go to Jordan to get a second opinion and it all happened rather quickly. The second and third opinions were identical. The X-rays showed that the cancerous cells had spread quickly and a mastectomy was the only option. I am undergoing chemotherapy now and my days are full of nausea, headaches, and vomiting. My long hair, which you stroked, is all gone. They say it will grow again after treatment, but I find that hard to believe right now. My chest scar has yet to heal, because I suffered an infection after the surgery. I woke up after surgery to find a big wound as if someone had stabbed me and stolen away the breast you so loved and called one of the domes of your pagan temple. The breast you used to cup with your palms. The breast whose nipple you used to suckle on at times and bite like an insatiable puppy at others. The breast whose rights you said you wanted to defend and which you wanted to liberate from the fabric and wires that strangle it. They took that breast away from me and it is no longer part of my body. I couldn't muster the courage to stand before the mirror—except once. I broke down afterward and cried for hours. I'm struck with the storms of irrational thoughts and feelings which inhabit anyone whose body is afflicted with sickness. *Why? Why me? I'm still too young for it. I'm not forty yet.* The doctor back in Baghdad said that cancer rates have quadrupled in recent years and it might be the depleted uranium used in the ordnance in 1991. I hate my body now and wish I could run away from it to a new body. I don't think I could live in peace with it. Forgive me for going on and on so selfishly about my fears and thoughts.

What I wanted to say is that I gave this a great deal of thought and only came to this decision because I love you and love your love for me. I never wanted that love to change. I know that you will read these lines and say that you will still love my body, even without my left breast. Don't lie! Even I no longer love my body and don't think I could ever love it again. I know you will always love me, but my fight with cancer might not end. This might seem harsh toward both of us, but I must sever myself from your life. I don't want you to live with a woman who has a ticking bomb in her body. Please forgive me for leaving without saying goodbye. I didn't want to say goodbye, but I will keep saying goodbye every day.

I will carry you in my memory. My body will carry your scents and pores in its memory.

Please forgive me. I will make things easier for us by not giving you my address and by giving you the opportunity to begin anew with another woman. I am already jealous of her without knowing who she might be.

This could very well be the most difficult sentence I have written in my whole life, but please don't try to get in touch with me.

Love and kisses,

Reem

I read the letter dozens of times until I had memorized every word. The first few times I wiped tears that fell. The tears kept falling afterward, but deep down inside. I felt they had amassed and settled in my chest and would remind me now and then that they were residing there forever. I tried to get her address, but to no avail. I heard that her father had come back for a few days and had given his lawyer full power of attorney and asked him to sell all their property. I heard later that they had settled in England. I asked Suha about her, but she said she hadn't heard anything either.

Months and years passed and my wound healed, but it left a scar I would touch from time to time. I used to reread the letter, which I hid in a small box together with an envelope containing some of our old letters and the photographs from our school days.

TWENTY-NINE

A few days after Hammoudy disappeared, Sayyid al-Fartusi visited me again. He said his heart sank when Hammoudy didn't pick up on his cell for five days and when he saw that the *mghaysil* was closed. He had stopped at Hammoudy's house and heard the news from his family. I invited him to come in.

He was visibly sad and looked worried as he drank the glass of water I brought him. He said he was willing to pay the ransom, no matter how much the figure was, if it turned out that Hammoudy had been kidnapped. What he added afterward revealed his fears of Hammoudy's inevitable fate: "God knows what happened to him. He doesn't deserve this." Then he recited *"With God alone rests the knowledge when the last hour will come and He sends down rain and knows what is in the wombs. No one knows what he will reap tomorrow and no one knows in what land he will die. Verily, God alone is all-knowing and all-aware."* He repeated the last verse twice and looked at the floor as if reading something written on it. He shook his head, saying, "There is no power save in God." Then he spoke of men.

"You know, whenever I think that humans have stooped to the lowest point, I discover that they can stoop even lower. The number of corpses thrown in garbage dumps and being fished out of the river has doubled in recent months. Even the dead are not safe anymore. They are booby-trapping corpses now."

This "they" everyone used nowadays in referring to the "other side" caught my attention. I was about to ask him who "they" were for him. Then I remembered that he had said on his first visit that he buried everyone irrespective of their sect or religion and that the remains of some of the bodies he buried must have belonged to the murderers who blew themselves up. Instead of asking him about "they," I wanted instead to know how and why he had started to do what he did.

"It's a long story."

"I have time."

He wasn't a practicing or pious Muslim when he was young, but what he saw during the withdrawal from Kuwait in 1991 transformed him completely.

"I never prayed or fasted. I even used to drink and was busy enjoying life. After graduating from college I was drafted into the army. A few months before finishing my service, Saddam invaded Kuwait and my unit was transferred there. When the war started, the bombing was continuous and hellish. I don't know how we survived. The only two who survived in my unit were myself and Musa, a soldier from Ammarah. We were together in the same trench. The others died and were buried in the sand.

"There was chaos from the start, because all communications and supply routes were cut off during the first few days of the war. We heard the decision to withdraw on the radio. Everyone was escaping on the highway toward Basra, because it was close to our units. Every moving object on that highway became a target for the fighter jets and bombers which were hovering and hunting humans as if they were insects. Musa said that to increase our chances of survival we should stay as far away as possible from the highway and the cars and vehicles, many of which were full of what the soldiers had looted. The Americans were firing at any vehicle. We ran like mad dogs for more than two hours without turning back.

"Musa's decision to abandon the highway saved our lives. Otherwise, we would've been charred like all the others I saw burning in their seats and whose remains were scattered all around us. The smell of burning flesh and hair made me sick and tortured me in nightmares for months afterward. I could never forget the smell or the sight of stray dogs devouring soldiers' bodies near Basra. I would stand there shocked and pick up a rock to throw at them, but Musa would violently pull me away, saying that it was useless because the dogs would return to their feast after we left. All we had with us were our water bottles, some dates in our pockets, and the pocket radio. We made sure not to use it too much to keep the batteries alive. Our goal was to get to Musa's relatives in Basra and sleep there until things calmed down and then we would go home.

"Our feet were swollen from running and walking the whole day. Basra's streets were empty when we got there. I saw graffiti on the walls saying 'Down with Saddam.' Some of his murals were defaced and smeared with paint. The news on the radio spoke of an uprising which started in Basra and spread all over the south after Bush called on Iraqis to 'take matters into their own hands.' You know the rest of the story. They changed the tune a few days later and no one in the world helped those who rose up. They started to call those who rose up hooligans, and then the Republican Guards units came and slaughtered thousands.

"We hid at Musa's relatives' for a week. The road to Baghdad was very dangerous. We heard about what they'd done to some of the Ba'thists, that they'd mutilated their bodies and hung some of them from electricity posts. I never liked the Ba'thists myself, and some members of my family had been executed by Saddam on mere grounds of suspicion, I swear to you. But it's a sin to do such things to any human being, even if he is your enemy. God will choose the appropriate torture for every oppressor. I thought I could just put all those scenes behind me, but those stray dogs followed me to Baghdad. Weeks after I returned, the nightmares started. I would see six or seven dogs tearing apart corpses, and whenever I tried to pick up a rock to throw it at them, it turned to dust. In another nightmare I would see my entire family being charred. When I'd try to pour water on them from my bottle, I'd discover that it was empty. I'd try to throw sand on them, but I would smell that stench again and wake up.

"I told my cousin about all these nightmares and the insomnia that ruined my days. He advised me to go to the mosque and pray. He was right, because prayer saved my mind and soul from the madness erupting all around me. Those dogs and the nightmares didn't disappear entirely, but they would return only once every six months or so. You asked about burying corpses, but the roots of all of this kept haunting me. I was assigned to work at the Ministry of Health. Through my job, I heard about the bodies abandoned at the morgue and other places because no one claimed them or bothered to bury them for whatever reason. That broke my heart. I told many friends and acquaintances about it. I knew there was a government cemetery, the Muhammad Sakran Cemetery, where the unknown were buried. I faced many obstacles at first when I started this project, but many do-gooders helped me out with donations and that's how it all started."

He asked whether I had changed my mind about working at the *mghaysil*, and I said that I hadn't. "God will reward you, you know," he assured me. I didn't respond, but asked him whether the dogs and nightmares were now leaving him in peace.

He laughed. "They left me alone, because they were afraid of what they saw in my other nightmares."

"What happens in these other nightmares?"

He laughed again: "I'll tell you some other time."

THIRTY

I'm walking in a public garden in Baghdad. I think I must have visited it a long time ago, since I recognize the path which goes through it and circles around the fountain. The fountain stands in the middle like a huge flower with petals of water. But I don't recall ever seeing so many white statues on the lawn: men, women, and children standing, sitting, or lying on the ground. The sky is ink blue and every now and then the moon hides behind flocks of clouds driven by the wind to an unknown fate. The wind appears to have moved one of the statues of a man, which stoops as if to look for something he's lost. I think I hear a groan. I approach the statue and the groans grow louder. I discover that the statue is shrouded in white. When I get closer, I hear a male voice begging me to sprinkle water on it.

"Who are you and why are you stooping like that," I ask.

"This is how I was when I died and I cannot move. Please, take me to the water, because I'm suffering."

I hold the figure by its shoulders, which are very cold, and drag it toward the fountain. I place it at the fountain's edge so that the water will spray the statue's head. The voice sighs and asks me to push it into the fountain's waters. I do. Before comprehending what has happened, I hear another groan and a voice saying "Me too, please."

THIRTY-ONE

Nine months before Hammoudy's disappearance, my mother started feeling severe pain in her stomach and was throwing up all the time. I took her to the doctor, who ordered numerous tests and prescribed some medicine. Her situation only got worse so I took her to a different doctor, who repeated the tests and then said she should have a colonoscopy. It turned out that she had a growth, but the biopsy determined that it wasn't malignant. It had to be removed, and the surgery went well. She was almost fully recovered when she got a severe infection and had to go back to the hospital for a month. The doctors' bills and the surgery and hospital expenses depleted everything I had saved from the money Hammoudy had given us every month. I had to borrow from my brother-in-law to pay the bills and cover other expenses. All my attempts to find a job failed. Job hunting in Baghdad had itself become a confounding quest through a labyrinth of checkpoints and walled neighborhoods.

The debts piled up. I was at wit's end and felt cornered, especially after Hammoudy's disappearance, which, aside from the deep emotional distress it caused, meant no steady income. Al-Fartusi came again to try to convince me to take up my father's work. He said it was not right to keep the *mghaysil* closed and urged me to open it and go back to work. He reminded me that the living had a debt and a responsibility to the dead. I didn't say no right away, and perhaps he felt that I was considering it, and that he had finally found a breach in my wall to dig through.

"You know that I'm not religious."

"It doesn't matter. What matters is intention." He invoked the

Qur'an again. "Piety does not consist in turning your faces toward the east or west.

"There are corpses scattered all over the streets and stuffed in fridges. If you purify them and shroud them, God will love you and forgive all your sins whether you pray or not. Plus, trust me, your father will be so pleased and his soul will be at rest in paradise."

"But I haven't washed in years and I may have forgotten all the details."

He smiled, as if sensing his victory, and said: "I don't believe you, but I can give you a book that contains every detail you need to know about the rules and rituals of washing and shrouding."

I don't know why I agreed. It was primarily the need for money, of course. I convinced myself that this would only be a temporary solution until I found a job or some other source of income. I never thought that I would keep on washing for months and years. Was there a mysterious force taking me back to the *mghaysil*? Did you have something to do with it, Father? Are you happy now?

Al-Fartusi hugged me and patted my shoulders before saying goodbye. He said he would get in touch with Mahdi, Hammoudy's nephew who'd been working with him, and tell him that the *mghaysil* would open again.

THIRTY-TWO

I see Reem standing in an orchard full of blossoming pomegranate trees. The wind moves the branches and the red blossoms appear to be waving from afar. Reem waves as well and her hands say: *Come close!* I walk toward her and call out her name, but I can hear neither my own voice nor the sound of my footsteps. All I hear is the wind rustling. Reem smiles without saying anything. I am much closer and I see two pomegranates on her chest instead of her breasts. She notices that I am looking at them and smiles as she cups them with her hands from below. Her fingernails and lips are painted pomegranate red. I rush toward her, and when I reach her and hug her, the left pomegranate falls to the ground. When I bend down to pick it up, I see red stains bathing my arm. I turn back and see Reem crying as she tries to stop the fountain of blood gushing from the wound.

THIRTY-THREE

"If your father were alive, he would be very happy."

My mother chattered excitedly as she prepared the *sufurtas* which she insisted I take to work with me, even though I had told her the night before that I would buy my lunch from one of the shops and that she shouldn't bother.

"Why would you want to eat outside food, son? Is there anything better than your mother's homemade food? I packed some chicken stew with potatoes and rice for you."

She was very pleased that I was going back to Father's work. I didn't tell her that the only reason was to be able to pay all the debts from her illness. She kissed me on the forehead and enlisted "God, Muhammad, and Ali" to accompany me and protect me.

Mahdi was slouching against the wooden door of the *mghaysil* with his knee bent and his right heel on the door itself. His hands were clasped over his chest. He was fifteen, with very short brown hair, hazel eyes, and thick eyebrows. His nose was big, and fuzz had already started to appear above his lips and on the sides of his face. He was thin, but with broad shoulders and a strong frame, which enabled him to lift bodies. He was wearing black sneakers, jeans, and a black jacket over a red-and-blue striped jersey with "Barcelona" written on the front.

We had agreed to meet at eight in the morning in front of the *mghaysil*. He straightened up when he saw me and moved away from the door. He greeted me with a smile and was a bit shy. I extended my hand and he shook it, calling me "Ustadh Jawad." I told him that *ustadh* wasn't necessary. I took the key out of my pocket and put it inside the lock to open the door. I thought to myself that he should be in school and not working with me—or with anyone else. He said that he had left school two years ago to support his family. He used to sell sandwiches and soft drinks, then worked with his uncle until his disappearance. His voice trembled as he mentioned the disappearance.

"Let's hope he will come back," I said, even though I had lost all hope. I wondered where Hammoudy's body was now and what had been done to it. That unanswerable and haunting question pierced my heart again as I opened the door.

I hadn't been to the *mghaysil* in a long time, and the smell overwhelmed me again. It's strange how some places can retain the same smell for decades. That morning the scent of stale air mingled with the distinct mixture of humidity, camphor, and lotus. I told Mahdi to go in ahead of me, but he hesitated out of respect, so I pushed him gently by the shoulder. He went in and stood on the right, waiting. I closed the door behind us.

The morning light looked as if it had retreated outside. I saw the marble washing bench from afar. It was wet with darkness. The timid sun could smuggle only a few rays through the high window. I walked to the end of the corridor. I turned the ceiling fan on and then went to the side door, which led to the small garden where the pomegranate tree stood. I opened it to let some fresh air in. I asked Mahdi to open the window in the side room so the place could breathe in more fresh air. I looked outside and saw the pomegranates dangling down. The cool September air began to fill the place, and I changed my mind about taking off my jacket. I told Mahdi that he was welcome to pluck the pomegranates later and take them home.

"You don't like them?" he asked.

"I do," I said, "but not from this tree."

I went to the cupboards and opened the doors. Everything was in its place just the way father used to have it. There were many bags of ground lotus leaves, but only a few camphor bags. I guessed that was why Hammoudy had gone to Shorja, but there was enough to last for the next few days. The white towels and shrouds were in their place, but the shrouds were packed in nylon bags and had supplications printed on them. There was plenty of cotton and bars of the olive colored soap, whose scent filled my nostrils. The pots and buckets were all neatly stacked.

I opened the faucet and the water gurgled, then came out in a rush. I stood at the washing bench and ran my fingers along its edges. It was as cold as the bodies that lie on it. I looked at my fingertips and saw the dust. I asked Mahdi to sweep the place. He went to the storage room to get the broom. I went to the side room. Everything was the same. The chairs, table, and the painting of Imam Ali right there next to the window. He had a yellow halo around his head with its green headdress. His eyebrows rose a bit and his brown eyes were darkened with kohl. The hair of his moustache and beard was wavy, and he was wearing a white shirt.

To the right of Imam Ali was a black-and-white photograph of Father, which Hammoudy must have put up. I asked my mother later where he had gotten the photograph and she said that he had asked for one to enlarge, but she had forgotten to tell me. In the photograph, Father had half a smile on his face and wore a white shirt with an open collar. I said to him: "*Here I am, back at the place you wanted me to inherit. I am taking your place, just as you took your father's. But I am warning you, father, I will not be here for long.*"

I heard the broom scraping the floor and a few minutes later dust particles found their way to my nose. I sat on the chair and looked at Imam Ali's picture again. I heard the voice of Muzaffar al-Nawwab clamoring in one of his poems where he addresses Ali: "*If you were to return now, your followers would fight against you and call you a Communist.*"

I took from my pocket the notebook in which, one summer many years ago, I had written down everything about washing bodies. Its pages had yellowed, but the cover was still intact. Sketches of my father's face and his worry beads and Imam Ali's face and the faces of other people filled the pages and framed the notes I'd taken.

Those notes were now older than Mahdi. I read one of them. "Before washing, we say 'I wash this corpse of this dead man as a duty and to seek God's favor.' During washing we must repeat: 'Forgiveness, O Lord,' or 'O Lord, this is the body . . . etc.'" I had written every little detail down in this notebook. Washing wasn't difficult or complicated. I had watched my father do it hundreds of times and had helped him.

Mahdi finished cleaning and asked what he should do next. I asked him to close the windows and doors, because it was getting cold, and to go to the women's *mghaysil* and get us some lotus and camphor just in case. He came back and stored the stuff in the cupboards, then stood at the door. I invited him to sit down. He took off his jacket and put it on the back of the chair. I wanted to get to know him better and asked him about his hobbies.

He said he loved soccer and played whenever he had a chance and that he wanted to be a professional player in the future.

"Why not?" I said and smiled. I pointed to his Barcelona jersey and asked whether he wanted to play for them.

"Yes," he said excitedly.

"What about Iraqi teams?"

"I am a Talaba fan."

I had stopped following the league, but told him that I was a diehard Zawra' fan. "What position do you like to play?"

"Striker."

Before we could chat any more, death knocked on the door. Mahdi got up and went to open it. My heart raced and I stayed in the chair for a few seconds. I heard Mahdi saying, "Yes, it's here." I got up, went and stood by the bench, then went to the corridor. Mahdi came back, followed by three men carrying a sheet hiding the dead man. Mahdi pointed to the washing bench and they laid the body there. He then pointed to me and told them, "Ustadh Jawad is the washer." The sentence had a strange effect on my ears. As if Mahdi had decreed what I would be doing.

"My condolences," I said. "What is he to you?"

"My nephew. My sister's son."

"May God have mercy on his soul. Can I see the death certificate?"

He asked one of the younger men with him to get it from the car. Mahdi started to fill the buckets with water. The man asked about the fees. I spontaneously repeated what my father used to say: "Whatever you can manage, plus the cost of the shroud, but later. The coffin is donated by the endowment, but we will deal with this later."

"Fine," he said.

I asked them to take a seat. The third man did so, but the deceased's uncle stood still. The young man came back and handed the death certificate to the uncle, who gave it to me with some hesitation. I looked at it. "Full Name: Jasim Muhammad 'Alwan. Sex: Male. DOB: 8-5-1982. Cause: Poisoning. Drug overdose/pills."

I handed it back to him without a word. The dead man was only twenty-four and had died before his life had even started. Drugs had become rampant, especially among young men and teenagers. The young man who brought the death certificate went and sat on the visitors' bench next to the other one.

I approached the washing bench and remembered that I had to take off my shoes and that I hadn't brought slippers from home. I was a bit flustered. I went to the side room and took off my shoes and socks. I put my socks inside the shoes and hid them under the chair. I could feel how cold the floor was. I rolled up my sleeves and went back to the washing room and headed to the faucet. The water was bitterly cold. I washed my hands and arms with soap and dried them with a towel Mahdi had prepared.

I stood to the right of the bench and removed the sheet from the dead man's face and body. He was naked except for white underpants. His skin was yellowish. He had short brown hair, a wide forehead, and a pointed nose. There was a mole on his right cheek next to his moustache. His lips were dry and looked thirsty. He had scattered patches of hair on his chest between the nipples. They narrowed to a line trailing down his belly. He was wire-thin. His bones and ribs were visible. I put my arm under his neck to lift him and pull the sheet from under his body. I got goose bumps.

I rested his head on the bench again. Mahdi put his hands under the dead man's knees to lift the rest of his body. I pulled away the remainder of the sheet and gave it to Mahdi, who folded it and handed it to the uncle. Mahdi brought me another white towel and handed it to me. He held a pair of scissors in his other hand. I put the towel over the man's waist and took the scissors from Mahdi. I lifted the towel a bit without showing anything and started to cut away his underwear from the side. I went around and did the same to the other side. I removed the underwear and gave it to Mahdi, who put it in a plastic bag he had brought and gave it to the uncle. I returned the scissors to Mahdi and then placed the palms of my hands on the dead man's belly and rubbed gently. It felt like hard plastic. I filled a bowl with water and poured some on his face. I inserted my index finger into his mouth and rubbed his teeth. Mahdi had started mixing in the ground lotus, which formed a foam and spread a pleasant smell. I poured another bowl of water over the man's head and washed his face. I looked at Mahdi and realized it was time to turn him on his side. We did so as I repeated, "Forgiveness, O Lord." I washed his right side from the head all the way down to the toes and repeated the same thing on his left side. Then we washed him again with water and camphor and then a third time with pure water.

For half an hour the only sounds were the splash of water and what I muttered. We dried him and shrouded him and put two branches of palm in the coffin.

After two years of work alongside Hammoudy, Mahdi had mastered the tasks of the assistant and the rhythms of washing. He was always ahead of me, anticipating the next step and preparing for it. This lessened my anxiety that I would do something wrong. When we went to the corner to fetch the coffin, the two young men got up. We put it on the ground next to the bench and placed the body in it. The uncle asked again about my fees and I told him that there was no set figure. He gave me ten thousand dinars. I thanked him and offered my condolences once again. They carried away the coffin and left.

I asked Mahdi about the amount as I put the bills in my pocket.

He said it was very good and that Hammoudy used to ask for twenty thousand if the deceased's family wanted the special shroud with the fancy print and supplications. I suggested we wash the bench and rearrange the bowls. He said he would do it himself.

I looked for the radio in the side room, but couldn't find it. Mahdi said he didn't know anything about a radio. I decided to bring a small one from home to keep us company. I realized that I'd forgotten to say, "I wash this corpse . . . " I sensed that Imam Ali was looking at me from the painting, but I didn't detect any censure or anger in his eyes.

Death was kind to me on my first day and gave me a long rest. No one else came until noon. I remembered the *sufurtas* and the food my mother had prepared for me. Mahdi hadn't brought any food with him. I gave him some money and asked him to get us two falafel sandwiches from Abu Karima's and to get two cans of soda, too. He smiled and seemed eager to go on the errand.

I sat waiting for him and leafed through my old notebook again. I found a few empty pages and decided to write down the names of the dead I was going to wash. I wrote the date and then "Jasim."

Names filled one notebook after the other in the days and months that followed.

THIRTY-FOUR

I cannot wake up from this endless nightmare of wakefulness. Some people go to work behind a desk on which papers are piled. Others operate machinery all day. My desk is the bench of death. The Angel of Death is working overtime, as if hoping for a promotion, perhaps to become a god. I walk down the street and look at people's faces and think *Who among them will end up on the bench next for me to wash?*

Every day of the week was difficult, but Thursday was the day al-Fartusi's refrigerated truck arrived with the weekly harvest of death: those who were plucked from their families and lives, tossed into the garbage in Baghdad's outskirts, thrown into the river, or rotting in the morgue. Most of them had no papers or IDs and no one knew their names. Instead of names, I wrote down the causes of death in my notebook: a bullet in the forehead, strangulation marks around the neck, knife stabs in the back, mutilation by electric drill, headless body, fragmentation caused by suicide bomb. Nothing could erase the faces. My memory became a notebook for the faces of the dead. I was on my way home one day when I realized that aside from Mahdi and my mother, I was living my days exclusively with the dead.

THIRTY-FIVE

On a February morning in 2006, I was getting dressed to go to work when I heard my mother wailing downstairs. I ran down barefoot and saw her sitting in front of the TV beating herself and crying, "O God, O God."

"What's wrong, mother? What happened?" I asked as I held her hands and begged her to stop. On the TV were images of a destroyed mosque.

Through her tears she said, "They bombed the Askari shrine. I wish God had blinded me so I wouldn't see it like that."

I tried to calm her down. I, too, felt sad, but for different reasons. I had visited the shrine in Samarra more than once. That is where the Mahdi is said to have disappeared and gone into occultation to return at the end of time. I had felt awe and sadness when I was inside it and could still see my mother crying as she held on to the golden window surrounding the mausoleum. I was quite young· back then and she had stood behind me and had kept me close so that I wouldn't get lost in the crowds. I felt the cold window as my cheek pressed against it. I felt the warmth of my mother's body pressing me from behind as she muttered her supplications and prayers. She cried as she mentioned Ammoury's name and then mine and my sister's and asked the imam to protect us. I cried along with her. All those pleas and tears did not work. Not for Ammoury. When we were in school we used to go on trips to Samarra to visit the spiral ziggurat. We would climb all the way to the top and look out at the golden dome of the shrine. It looked like a star that has fallen from the sky and now rested on earth after being dipped in golden water.

The band at the bottom of the TV screen scrolled by with condemnations and statements from every side. I realized that matters would deteriorate even further. Corpses would pile up everywhere. My mother was afraid that other domes would be blown up. "Who can stop them if they want to blow up al-Kazim. God help us!"

"God help us, but please take it easy and calm down. They won't blow up al-Kazim."

"I don't want to calm down. You are way too calm about this. Didn't they fire rockets at it a few months ago? Aren't there explosions every year during 'Ashura? You just don't care about Shiites."

I was about to tell her that she was right in a way. I had come to a point where I hated everyone equally, Shiites and Sunnis alike. All these words were suffocating me: Shiite, Sunni, Christian, Jew, Mandaean, Yazidi, infidel. If only I could erase them all or plant mines in language itself and detonate them. But here I was, slipping into the very same language of bombing and slaughter.

"Thank you mother," I said. I went upstairs, got dressed and made my way out of the house. When she heard my footsteps she said, "Godspeed, son," but I didn't answer.

When I came home that evening she kissed my forehead and apologized.

"What can I do, son. My heart was scorched."

"There is no heart in this country that isn't crushed, mother."

We had tea in front of the TV. The daily harvest of news was the same stuff I had heard on the radio all day: responding to a statement by the grand cleric al-Sistani, angry demonstrations took place in Baghdad, Najaf, and Basra. There were lethal attacks on five Sunni mosques in Baghdad, and mosques in other cities were torched. I looked at my mother. "What do you expect?" she said. "Their hearts are scorched."

"So they go burn mosques because their hearts are scorched?"

She probably figured that if we got into an argument I would just leave and go to the Internet café, so she retreated by saying, "You are right. Even if they drew blood first, one shouldn't burn a place of worship."

The government declared three days of official mourning. As for the sectarian killings, they spread without any official announcements and lasted well beyond the three days. The satellite channels were buzzing with noise and sectarian frenzy on both sides. They hosted many turbaned men, most of whom were experienced in fanning the flames of hatred and rousing other zealots of their sects, especially masked ones, to translate what was being said with their weapons and eloquent daggers. The next day more than a hundred bodies were found all around Baghdad. The rate of corpses delivered to the *mghaysil* didn't increase, but I thought of my Sunni comrades on the other side of this valley whose hours were now choked with death and water.

My uncle sent an e-mail asking whether things were all right with us. He reminded me of what he had said three years earlier when he visited. He had said that the hell of sectarianism was inevitable and that helmets and turbans would sever heads and burn everything in sight. He reiterated his offer to help me if I still intended to emigrate or to continue my studies abroad as I had told him when he was in Baghdad. I wrote back and told him that I was thinking about it, but my mother's fate, if I were to leave, was paralyzing me.

THIRTY-SIX

A deep voice says: "Remove the blindfold."

At a desk in front of me sits a man whose features I can't make out in the blinding light.

He asks, "Is your name Jawad Kazim?"

"Yes."

He looks at some papers in front of him and reads: "Graduated Academy of Fine Arts. Failed sculptor. Painter. Are you a believer?"

Bewildered by his question, I say, "Excuse me?"

He screams: "Motherfucker. Don't try to be a smart ass with me. You understand the question very well. Are you a believer?"

"Yes, thank God, I am."

He motions to the man standing next to me. The latter punches me so hard I fear my head will fall off.

"You piece of shit! You haven't fasted or prayed or gone to a mosque in a hundred years and you say you are a believer? How could you desecrate the bodies of martyrs when you are a dirty apostate? Why are you meddling in this profession anyway if you are an artist?"—He says "artist" sarcastically and in a different tone—"It's better for you to scribble away and play with your mud or shit. Go get drunk and fuck around with your faggot artist friends, but don't touch the bodies of honorable men, you piece of shit. I'll tear your ass apart."

His phone rings. "I'll teach you," he says, then answers his phone and starts chatting and joking with a friend, making plans for dinner.

I woke to the ringing of my phone.

THIRTY-SEVEN

Three months after the bombing of the al-Askari mosque I went home after work and found my mother and some relatives sitting in the guest room. I was tired and wanted just to say a quick hello. The door was ajar. I saw a familiar face—a female cousin whom I had seen a few years before at a wedding. A much younger and very beautiful girl who resembled her sat between her and a boy of about ten. When I knocked at the door, the woman covered her head with a black scarf, but the girl smiled at me and kept her head uncovered. We exchanged greetings and I welcomed them.

"Do you remember Um Ghayda'?" asked my mother.

"Yes, of course," I said.

"And this is her lovely daughter Ghayda' and her son Ghayth."

I welcomed them again, then excused myself and went to the kitchen to get some food. My mother followed me and said she wanted to discuss something. Um Ghayda' and her children were in a tight spot. "They can't stay at their own house in 'Amiriyya," she said, "because of all the threats they're getting and all the killing over there. Her husband was killed five months ago, and she is alone. She wants to stay with us until things calm down, since our neighborhood is safe for Shiites."

I said that it was fine by me. My mother kissed me on my cheek, saying, "I was afraid you'd be upset."

I didn't spend much time at home to start with, especially since getting addicted to the Internet. I knew that the house had become too empty for my mother after my father's death. My sister rarely visited. I thought that the company of Um Ghayda' might cheer her up. The guest room was big enough for the three of them to sleep in. It turned out later that Um Ghayda' had back pains, so my mother invited her to sleep with her in her bed. Ghayda' and Ghayth slept in the guest room on mattresses that Ghayda' would spread at night and pick up in the morning.

I wasn't averse to solitude, but their presence restored some life to our house, especially when we gathered for dinner at night in front of the TV. I noticed also that my mother's mood was much better than before. Her sighs and complaints decreased. She listened less often to the Shiite lamentation tapes that were popular at the market, and whose singers could sometimes be seen on the satellite channels as well. I explained to her that the death I saw every day from morning till evening was enough for me. I wanted to come home not to more mourning but merely to some peace of mind.

THIRTY-EIGHT

I am washing the corpse of a skinny old man with white hair and a wrinkly face and forehead. My mind wanders. The man opens his eyes, shakes his head, and tries to get up. The small bowl falls from my hand and I retreat from the bench in fear.

He says in a hoarse voice, "I didn't think that I would have to do this myself, but you can't focus and keep thinking of silly shit." He picks up the bowl, fills it with water, and pours it on his head. He reaches for the ground lotus. I try to give him a hand, but he refuses and tells me to go away and sit down.

Dozens of corpses start coming from every direction. Some come through the main door, others from the side door which leads to the small garden. Some come out of the storage room. Some wear nothing but a cloth around the waist. Others are shrouded and trying to shed their shrouds as they approach the washing bench. Corpses begin to wash one another and others stand in line around the bench awaiting their turns. Their numbers multiply and they fill the entire *mghaysil*, leaving no place for me. I go out into the street, but throngs of living corpses are surrounding the place, filling the streets and sidewalks. I start to suffocate, then bolt awake.

THIRTY-NINE

The restaurant that Abu Ghayda' had co-owned on the road to al-Taji military camp had been bombed by the Americans at the beginning of the war. He used to joke that the hot spices and pickled mango he used in his falafel sandwiches were at the top of the Pentagon's list of weapons of mass destruction that threatened the world. He and his partner repaired the restaurant and reopened it four months later, but business was slow. That area had become a battleground for the Americans and the armed men who attacked them. Abu Ghayda' lost everything and was forced to close shop.

After spending a year unemployed, he read ads for well-paying jobs at the Ministry of Interior. He went to Nusoor Square early one morning and stood in line to register his name. A suicide bomber standing in line with all the others blew himself up. By the time Um Ghayda' got to the hospital, Abu Ghayda' had shut his eyes forever.

Um Ghayda' cried whenever she remembered her husband and told the story of his death. "Isn't it a crime?" she would ask. "The man was standing in line to find a job to support his family. Is this their honorable resistance? If they want to kill the occupiers, why come after us?"

Young Ghayda' joined in her mother's tears whenever her father was mentioned. As for Ghayth, he would just drown in silence and pretend to watch TV, but the sorrow was visible in his eyes. His semipermanent silence worried me. What was he thinking of? His mother tried to overcompensate for the absent father by buying him whatever game he wanted, and by showering him with kisses and love. He was embarrassed by her attention when we were around, especially when she pinched what she called his "apple-y cheeks."

Ghayda' was nineteen. Notwithstanding the sadness in her honey eyes, her face was full of life, and her laughter lit up our gatherings. Her hair was chestnut brown, wavy, but short, exposing her beautiful neck. Her eyebrows and lashes were thick like her mother's—but unlike her mother's carefully plucked. Her lips were full, and when she was shy or embarrassed, she would bite the lower one.

Ghayda' had finished high school with good grades and had been admitted to the English Department at the College of Arts in Mosul, but her parents had refused to let her go. It was too dangerous for her to travel and live there alone while the bombings and massacres continued. Her father was unsuccessful in transferring her to Baghdad or al-Mustansiriyya University, so she lost the year.

Her lively presence spread an air of beauty, femininity, and life, a welcome contrast to those long days washing male bodies to make ends meet, and an incentive to return home in the evening. I started to pay more attention to my looks and my clothes.

FORTY

One of Giacometti's statues lies on the washing bench. I assume I am meant to wash it. As I pour water over its tiny head, the sculpture dissolves into tiny fragments. I put the bowl aside and try to pick up the pieces and repair the damage, but everything disintegrates in my hands.

FORTY-ONE

One night I woke up from one of my nightmares around three in the morning. I couldn't fall asleep and kept tossing and turning. I was thirsty so I went downstairs to get a glass of water. I noticed that the electricity was on so I tiptoed to the living room to watch TV. I kept the volume very low and started surfing the channels. Ten minutes later, I heard footsteps. Ghayda's face appeared in the dark.

"Is it OK if I watch with you?" she whispered.

"Of course, come in." I apologized for waking her, but she said she was an insomniac.

"You are still too young for insomnia," I said.

She smiled. "You have insomnia too?"

"Oh yes, chronic."

She was barefoot and wore light blue sweatpants and a white T-shirt without a bra. She sat on the couch on the right-hand side, put her feet up, and hugged her knees. I could see the area between her armpit and the slope of her breast. The announcer on one of the satellite channels was recapping the day's news. I changed the channel half a minute later to an old Egyptian film.

"Thank you for letting us stay here, by the way," she said.

"Not at all . . . my mother is very happy to have you here."

She surprised me by asking: "And you?"

"I am happy too," I said. "I hope you are comfortable and all?"

"Very. It's the difference between heaven and hell. There are no shots fired at night here. No threats and no headaches, but I'm sad, because all my books are still back home."

"Which books? Schoolbooks?"

"No, novels and stuff."

"I have a lot of books in my room. You are welcome to them. If things calm down we can go to your house and retrieve some of the books."

"Really? Thanks, that would be super."

"Sure, tomorrow I'll lend you some, or you can go in yourself and choose."

"Thanks so much." After some silence she said, "Can I ask you a question?"

"Of course."

"Are you doing all right with your work?"

It was surprising. Few people ever bothered to ask. My uncle inquired in his letters, and so did Professor al-Janabi. All my mother ever said was, "May God give you more strength."

"Why do you ask?"

She smiled and bit her lower lip and said, "Never mind. I'm sorry. I shouldn't have asked."

"No, not at all."

"It's just that I see how stressed out you are when you come home. Even though you laugh with us, it's obvious that you're totally drained."

"Well, frankly speaking, it's very difficult, psychologically."

Her smile had disappeared and she said, "I'm really sorry," in a genuine tone.

"Thanks for asking."

She didn't ask any other questions about my work that night. We chatted about many things in a hushed voice until dawn. She started to yawn and so did I. I excused myself, saying that I had to get a couple of hours of sleep to make it through the day at work.

"I'm sorry for keeping you up."

"I'm not—I had fun."

"Me too."

"Sweet dreams."

"You too."

As I walked upstairs I smiled to think that Ghayda' and I were becoming closer. Then I stopped smiling: no matter how innocent our time together, our mothers would interpret it quite differently.

FORTY-TWO

He was in his early fifties. He had burn scars on his forehead
and right cheek. A bit chubby and bald except for a few scattered
white hairs on the sides of his head and a white moustache. His
hazel eyes stared at me through black-rimmed glasses. He said that
the people at the morgue had sent him my way and that he had a
corpse he wanted to wash and bury right away.

"May God have mercy on his soul. Is he a relative of yours?"

"No, I have no idea who he is."

I must have looked surprised, and he added, as we walked to his
car: "You won't believe me if I tell you what happened to me."

"What happened?"

"It's a long and very strange story."

I didn't push him further. In the past two years I had seen and
heard unimaginable things. He handed me the death certificate. In
the blank for the name was written "anonymous." The cause of
death was severe burns, the date two months before. He pointed to a
white car parked nearby. A man was seated behind the wheel, but
the trunk was open. I saw a thick bag of nylon, of a type often used
for anonymous corpses, with its sides stapled. Despite the thickness
of the nylon and the many layers of wrapping, I could see that the
corpse was charred.

"I can't wash it if the burns are severe: it'll disintegrate. We just
do *tayammum*."

"Is that what you people usually do?"

I wasn't sure who was meant by "you people"—washers or Shiites
—so I asked him: "What do you mean?"

"Look, brother, I'll be honest with you. I'm not a Shiite."

"Why did you bring him here, then?"

"He is a Shiite. Didn't I tell you it's a strange story you would never believe?"

He sounded like he was dying to tell me the story.

"If the corpse is too mutilated, burned, or swollen so that washing is difficult and could make it disintegrate, it is not compulsory to wash it," I said. "Why don't you tell me your story?"

"I'm a taxi driver trying to make a living. I live in al-Sayyidiyya and I picked up this poor man—" he made a gesture with his hands that added to the sadness in his voice. "He seemed like a good and honest man. We started yapping about this miserable situation we are in and about the massacres and politics of it all. The whole thing about Shiites and Sunnis came up and he said he was a Shiite. We argued a bit, but we were in agreement and were consoling each other. I had to take a leak and I asked to stop for a minute. I parked the car on the side next to the trees on al-Qanat Highway. There were choppers hovering overhead that day. Something had happened in al-Sadr City between the Americans and the Mahdi Army.

"I'd just unzipped my pants when I heard a huge explosion. It was so strong I thought my eardrum had burst. I looked back and saw that my car had become a ball of fire. I ran back and saw an American Apache up in the air whirling and heading back toward my car. I didn't know what to do and was afraid it would fire at me too. There was no fire extinguisher, so I started to grab dirt and throw it at the car. I ran and stood in the middle of the street, waving to cars with both hands. I wanted someone to stop and help me, but no one did. I was screaming at the top of my voice 'Please help! People . . . Please.'" I thought I should try to open the door to get him before the car exploded. I took off my shirt and wrapped it around my hand. I opened the door. The fire flew at me, burning my head, my forehead, my cheek." He pointed to his cheek. "I don't know how I managed to pull him out. He was in flames. I dragged him away and kept trying to put out the fire with my shirt and with dirt. He was already charred and I could smell his burned flesh and hair.

"The car exploded and parts of it scattered everywhere. I don't remember how long I sat there dazed. I started to walk and wave to cars, but no one stopped. They must've thought that I was crazy, because I was half-naked. I walked for a whole hour before some guy stopped and drove me home. God bless him. My neighbor took me to the hospital to treat my burns. I reported the incident, but no one explained why the Americans had fired at the car. They told me to file a petition for compensation and I did, but it's all talk. Nothing came out of it. The face of that man who was charred kept haunting me.

"I called the police and told them a man's corpse was out there on the street, that they had to pick it up before dogs ate it. They said, 'We can't do it. We don't have enough personnel.' Can you believe it? But I should've known. If we, the living, are worthless, then what are the dead worth? So I went with my brother—he's the one who drove me here today—to see whether there was anything left of the car or whether they'd picked him up. But he was still lying out there. I just couldn't stand it, so we put him in the trunk and took him to the morgue. They have piles there in their fridges and no one knows where their families are, and they are running out of space. They take their pictures, I'm sure you know about it, and save them on the computer and wait for someone to come by and recognize them so they can be taken away and buried.

"This man was in the morgue for two months and no one asked about him. Isn't it a sin not to bury him? I told them I would take him and see that he was buried and pay for the whole thing. I signed the papers. I can't take him all the way to Najaf. It's way too dangerous, but they said there was a new cemetery for the unknown that I could take him to. So we brought him here to you."

I took a deep breath and said "God bless you. There are still good people in this world." I said goodbye to him.

In the evening I told his story to Um Ghayda' and my mother in the hopes of changing their opinions and judgments about "them," the Sunnis.

It was useless.

FORTY-THREE

My eyes began to meet Ghayda's quite often. Only her brother noticed the dialogue of our eyes when others were around, and he never said a word.

I fulfilled my promise and chose a few novels to lend her. When I gave her the books, our hands touched, and I felt a surge of blood in my veins. She had started to help my mother with the housecleaning. I noticed that the desk in my room, which was usually covered with old newspapers, papers, and books, was neat and nice. So she was going into my room. She asked me once about my painting, and when I asked how she'd known, she mentioned seeing a painting in my room which bore my signature. It was a variation on Giacometti and depicted a naked, wire-thin woman walking toward a white horizon.

I told her that that was a long time ago and was the heedlessness of youth. She laughed and said that the heedlessness of youth was quite beautiful. She asked why I stopped painting. That, I said, was a long story for another day.

I found myself sketching her face and body in my notebook of the dead to distract myself. It was a way of running away from death, running toward her. Then I felt guilty for imprisoning her body with the names of the dead, so I set aside a new notebook for her alone and started taking it with me to work every day. From memory, I sketched her painting her toenails. I had happened to see her doing that through the guest room door. Her legs were crossed and her right leg was exposed all the way above her knee, revealing her smooth thigh. We looked into each other's eyes and she smiled without moving or changing her position.

We had three or four more nocturnal encounters. While the house was asleep, we traded stories and worries. Some of her questions were gutsy. One night she asked me about my relationships, so I told her all about Reem. She was moved by the story's sad end, and I thought I sensed a bit of jealousy as well. So I asked her about relationships.

She laughed and said: "I'm a good girl and don't have relationships." She added that she hadn't had the chance, because she was kept from college and had had only teenage relationships—"nothing but chatter."

I was taken by her intelligence and her maturity. She also gave me hope, because despite what her family had suffered in the civil war and sectarian clashes, she hadn't been swept into blaming the Sunnis for everything and jumping over history as our mothers often did. She would side with me when I argued with them. She even stood against her mother when Um Ghayda' said that Shiites hadn't ruled for fourteen hundred years, and that Saddam's regime had been Sunni. Ghayda' reminded her that the Americans had made a deck of cards with pictures of the most-wanted officials from the previous regime, and that the number of Shiites in the deck was larger than the number of Sunnis.

Um Ghayda' often repeated that the Sunnis cannot stand Shiites being in power and have always wanted to slaughter them. I reminded her of the Sunnis who jumped into the river to save the Shiites who were drowning the day of the A'imma bridge accident. Or Shiite militias which torched Sunni mosques. Or the stories of the secret prisons where Sunni prisoners were tortured with electric drills. I harped on all the Ba'thists who were Shiites, Kurds, and Christians, and ended with my favorite example of the corrupt ex-minister of information, al-Sahhaf, and asked her: "Wasn't he a Shiite?"

She raised her eyebrows and said: "Oh my. Are you with us or with them?"

"Don't you know he's the defense lawyer for Sunnis?" my mother told her.

"I'm all by myself. Neither with you nor with them," I said. I kept silent after that time and tried to avoid such useless arguments.

My uncle asked me in an e-mail for news about sectarian clashes. I said that I felt as if we had been struck with an earthquake which had changed everything. For decades to come, we would be groping our way around in the rubble it left behind. In the past there were streams between Sunnis and Shiites, or this group and that, which could be easily crossed and were even invisible at times. Now, after the earthquake, the earth had all these fissures, and the streams had become rivers. The rivers became torrents filled with blood, and whoever tried to cross, drowned. The images of those on the other side of the river had been inflated and disfigured. And out of these rivers came creatures which were extinct, or so we had thought. Old myths returned to cover the sun with their darkness and to crush it into pieces. Now each sect or group had a sun, moon, and world of its own. Concrete walls rose to seal the tragedy.

FORTY-FOUR

My desire for Ghayda' increased every day. I felt that she was
drawn to me, too, but I never mustered enough courage to make a
move. I didn't want to complicate my life and stir up family problems. My intense desire gave free rein to my imagination. My body
would thirst for her and be watered by her. It would flow and drown,
for her. All while I was asleep in my own bed, which I never thought
I might share with her one day.

I woke up one night from a nightmare feeling thirsty. As usual,
there was no electricity, so I lit a candle and took it downstairs to the
kitchen. Ghayda' rushed toward me and I suddenly found her hugging me and burying her head in my chest, whispering "I'm scared,
Jawad, very scared." The candle fell and its flame went out. I put my
arms around her and asked her softly, "What is scaring you?"

"Nightmares."

I put my right hand on her head and caressed her hair and said,
"Don't be scared. It's over now."

Her breasts pressed against my chest and the warmth in her body
flowed into mine. I kissed her head and smelled the henna in her
hair. I felt my erection pushing against her. Her lips were kissing my
neck. She looked up. I kissed her forehead, but she lifted her head
higher and I felt she was on her toes. I wiped a few tears off her
cheek. She touched my left cheek. I kissed her wrist and felt her
warm breath on my chin.

I kissed her lips lightly and she responded. Our lips met more
forcefully. I sucked her upper lip voraciously while my hands caressed her back. She held onto me. My tongue wandered into her

mouth, and she gently bit it. I kissed her cheek and took her earlobe between my lips. She was tickled and swayed like a branch.

The trouble that would erupt if we were exposed flashed into my mind. Her brother was a few meters away and her mother just upstairs. I told myself that I had to stop before it was too late. I put my hand on her cheek. I kissed her one last time on the mouth and whispered in her ear, "I'm sorry."

She put her head on my chest and said, "I'm not."

I caressed her hair a bit and then said, "OK, good night."

She didn't answer. I left the kitchen and made my way upstairs in the dark. I got back into bed and was gripped by mixed feelings of pleasure and regret. I retrieved our images kissing and started to touch myself. I heard the door opening slowly and she was right there. She closed the door behind her. I got up and stood in front of her.

"I want to sleep next to you," she whispered.

I hugged her and we kissed. I locked the door and took her to my bed. I took her T-shirt off and kissed her between her breasts. She dropped her sweatpants and they fell at her feet. I touched her underwear and it was drenched. I pushed her to my bed and she lay on her back. I kissed her everywhere, compensating for the years I'd squandered. Her skin felt very soft, and warm to my tongue.

She took the initiative and explored my body with her fingers and mouth. When I took off her underwear she didn't stop me. She was shaved. I tried to kiss her in between her thighs, but she pushed my head away gently and whispered, "Not today."

With fingers and hands we made each other shudder, the need for silent secrecy increasing our ecstasy. Afterward, I had to be strict and tell her to go back to her bed before daybreak. She bit my lip and hurt me a bit as she said goodbye.

We had our own secret world every night between two and four in the morning, fleeing from our nightmares to each other's bodies. It was a world bordered by danger and the fear of scandal. One night she whispered coquettishly, "Do whatever you want with my body, but not from the front." It was reasonable for her to preserve her capital in a society like ours. The first part of what she said—"Do whatever you want"—triggered a volcano in my body. We did everything but fully unite our bodies. I played in the taboo zone with my finger and gave my offerings with my tongue.

Her nocturnal presence reminded me that life can be generous, if only for a few hours a day. I found myself singing out loud for the first time in years while I was walking home. I often wished that the entire world would dissolve, including our mothers, society and its traditions, and the entire country. I would look at my hand after touching her breast and could not believe that a few hours later it would touch the body of another man. Her naked body started to flash in my mind as I washed, and often I felt guilty.

"Take me," she would say. When I pretended not to know what she meant and asked "Where to?" she would say, "To you." I asked her once, "What do you want with me? I'm too old for you and will be a useless troll in twenty years." "Why do you think they invented Viagra?" she said and laughed wholeheartedly.

She liked to chat after we were done making love, but I wanted to feel the pleasure of emptiness—which never lasted long and which I felt should never be interrupted by anything. I was more concerned than she that we would be discovered, and I would urge her to go back to her room lest her brother wake up and find her gone. She would cling to me and say that he was a deep sleeper. She usually put two pillows under the blanket to make it look like she was there.

When my mother, who must've noticed that Ghayda' and I liked each other, asked me what I thought of her, I could smell a conspiracy to have us get married.

"Isn't she gorgeous?" she asked me.

"Yes, she is. Why?"

"Do you like her?"

"Why do you ask?"

"If you like her, I can ask her mom."

"Hold on a second. Who told you I wanted to get married?"

"What do you mean, son? Are you gonna be single forever? I wanna be happy before I die."

"You have a long life ahead of you."

She usually shook her head and put her hand on her cheek after these conversations.

My entire body was full of Ghayda', but my heart was full of death. She started to say "I love you." I would stay silent and just kiss her. She thought that I was still in love with Reem. More than once she asked, "Is she still in your heart?" I would answer her truthfully, "I don't have a heart anymore."

I told her that she should protect her heart. Should I have told her the truth? Did I know it? All I knew was that I was tired of myself and of everything around me. I knew that my heart was a hole one could pass through but never reside in. I desired her and wanted her and wanted to be with her, but I was drained. I was not material for marriage or a family.

Two and a half months after our bodies had met in the dark, Ghayda's maternal uncle called. He asked her mother to go to Amman with the children so he could arrange their asylum application. He lived in Sweden, which he told her was much more receptive to Iraqi refugees than other countries. He could serve as a guarantor. Ghayda' was unhappy.

She asked me again, "Don't you want me?"

This question killed me. "Yes," I said. "I want you, but I cannot get married."

"You're a coward," she said. It was the only time she ever insulted me.

For the first few weeks after they were gone, her scent lingered in my bed, but then I slowly returned to my habit of solitude. Should I have clung to her? Could I have? We talked on Skype a few times after they left. She would text message me every now and then.

Her voice sounded sad the last time we spoke on Skype. I had told her that I was thinking of leaving Iraq for good and that I might come to Amman in a month or two in order to get asylum or a scholarship. My mom was going to live with my sister. I thought this would make her happy since we would see each other soon, but she said nothing.

"Why are you silent?" I asked her.

"You used to be silent so often when we were together. Don't I have the right to be silent?" Then she added: "Our asylum application was accepted and we are going to Sweden in a few weeks to live with my uncle."

We were both silent and then she asked me a question I couldn't answer: "Why did you let me go?"

FORTY-FIVE

Mahdi and I were sitting in the side room when we heard knocks. Mahdi went to open the door. A voice murmured, confirming that this was the *mghaysil*. I got up and stood at the door. A man in his early fifties came in with two younger men who looked like him. He looked well to do and was carrying a black bag. I welcomed them.

"We have a dead man we want to wash and shroud," he said.

"Sure. Where is the corpse?" I asked.

One of the two young men lowered his head. The other looked at me. The older man extended the hand holding the black bag and said in a trembling voice: "We have only the head."

I stood silent for about twenty seconds and couldn't say anything. I had washed a corpse with its severed head a few months ago, but this was the first time I got a head by itself.

"God help you. I'm very, very sorry." I took the black sack from him and put it on the washing bench. It made a thud. I pointed to the bench next to the wall and asked them to sit there. The sorrowful young man said, "I'm gonna wait outside, Dad." The other young man walked over and sat on the bench, but the old man stood near the washing bench.

"How are you related?" I asked.

"He's my son."

"May God have mercy on his soul."

"May he have mercy on the souls of your dead."

I didn't ask him for the death certificate. I thought about asking him about the cause of death, but then changed my mind. It would only cause him more grief.

"What was his name?"

"Habib."

I went to the faucet and washed my hands and arms. I took out plenty of cotton and scissors and put them on the table near the cupboard. Mahdi washed his hands and arms and started to fill a big bowl with water. I took the scissors to the washing bench and started cutting through the sack from the top down. The right side of the head appeared. The black hair was kinky and dirty. The skin was pale yellow and his beard was unshaved. I put my hand inside the sack. The head felt like thick plastic and I was disgusted. I took the head out of the sack, but then didn't know how to place it on the washing bench. I tried to place it as if it were still attached to its body, but it tilted to the side, and its cheek rested on the bench.

The man sighed and said, "There is no power save in God Almighty." The young man sitting on the bench covered his eyes and lowered his head.

Mahdi put the bowl on a stool next to the bench and mixed in the ground lotus leaves. A lather formed and he put the small pouring bowl on the surface of the water. Mahdi was stunned as well, looking at the head. The edges of the severed neck were yellowish like the rest of the face. I could see the tattered skin tissue and flesh and the dried pink and gray ends of blood vessels. There was a huge scar on his right cheek and a black spot on his forehead. I had to turn the head to the other side so we could start washing its right side.

As I poured the water, I wondered about the torture he had suffered right before his head was severed. What was the last thought that went through his head? Could he see, or did they deprive him of the right to face his killers? Could he hear what they were saying? Why, and in what or whose name, did they sever it? Was he a victim of the sectarian war or just thugs?

The head was going to move if I didn't hold it myself. I asked Mahdi to pour the water. I repeated, "Forgiveness, forgiveness," and held the head with my left hand and scrubbed the hair on the right side with my right hand. I washed and scrubbed every part carefully from the forehead all the way to the neck, as Mahdi poured the water. A few clots of dried blood fell off the neck. I turned the head to the other side and repeated the scrubbing. As usual, we washed it once more with camphor and then with water alone. I dried it and put cotton in the nostrils and a lot of cotton around the neck, but it kept falling off. I decided to hold it in place later with a cloth.

Mahdi dried the bench. I put camphor on the forehead, nose, and cheeks. Mahdi brought the shroud. I folded it twice and placed it on the bench and sprinkled some camphor on it. I took the head and put it in the middle of the shroud. I asked Mahdi to cut a big piece of cloth to tie around the head. I held the head with my left hand and put one end of the cloth at the top and pressed down on it with my other hand. I asked Mahdi to put wads of cotton on the neck and hold it in place. I tied the cloth around the neck and the head twice and then put it under the chin. He was all covered in white except for the closed eyes, nose, mouth, and part of the cheeks. There was obviously no need for all three pieces of the shroud we usually use, so I just used a second one to wrap around the head and we tied it with a strap.

I was about to ask the old man whether they wanted a coffin, then realized how silly that might sound. Mahdi was looking at me, waiting for my signal, so I pointed to the corner where the coffins are stacked. We went there and brought one and put it on the floor. This was one of the few times I had not needed Mahdi's help to carry a man. During the past two years, I had carried the children I washed and put them in their coffins while Mahdi watched.

I carried the shrouded head and placed it in the coffin. I forgot to include a branch of pomegranate or palm. Mahdi brought the cover and I covered it and said to the old man, "God have mercy on his soul." The young man got up from the bench and approached. The old man thanked me and, after paying the fees, suddenly said, "Do you know what they did to him?"

"Who?" I asked.

"I don't know," he said and proceeded to tell me the story of the head and the man to whom it belonged.

"He was an engineer. They kidnapped him and for two weeks we didn't know anything about him. We went to every police station and hospital asking about him. One morning, we woke up and found this sack right at our doorstep. His mother found it. She opened it and had a nervous breakdown and hasn't been the same since. They had a note with it saying: 'If you want the rest you must pay twenty thousand U.S. Dollars. Call this number.' We called for two days, but no one answered. Finally someone answered and said to meet them right behind Madinat al-Al'ab. We borrowed and sold things, but could only get ten thousand. My two sons went to the meeting, and the kidnappers threatened them. They took the money and said they would deposit the rest of the body in front of the house, but they never showed up, and all we have is his head. Can you imagine? Which religion or creed allows such a thing? Does God allow this?"

"God help you and may God have mercy on his soul," was all I could say.

The young man urged his father to leave. "Let's go, Dad."

Mahdi helped them carry the coffin outside. We sat together in silence, neither of us wanting to say anything about the head. I added Habib's name to the new notebook I had started after filling the last one. Next to his name I wrote, "severed head."

FORTY-SIX

I was standing in a long line at the passport office. I had been banned from traveling long before, because my uncle was a Communist, and I couldn't believe that after all these years I was finally going to leave. I had finished everything, had paid the fees, and was waiting in front of the window to get the passport. There were scores of people ahead of me, but the pace was good. I felt guilty about leaving my mother alone and going off, but I just couldn't take it anymore.

I noticed that the young man standing in front of me was wearing a coat, even though it was warm. He kept turning and looking back at the line as if looking for someone. He looked at his watch a number of times. A few minutes later he stepped aside and put his hand into his coat pocket and pulled something which triggered a huge explosion. I felt his blood on my face and his body parts striking my body. Some of the bodies of those waiting in line were scattered. Corpses scattered around and I saw people running and screaming, but all I could hear was a strange whistle. I touched my body and was astonished that it was intact. I ran to the exit and out to the street. I headed to the *mghaysil* and opened the faucet to wash myself. I lay down on the washing deck to die, but instead I awoke.

FORTY-SEVEN

I was just about ready to lock the *mghaysil* and go home after a
bloody day. I thought it was strange for Mahdi to have left without saying goodbye. Suddenly, five men carrying machine guns stormed the
place and surrounded me. Two grabbed me, tied my wrists behind
my back, and held me fast. The others began to search the entire
place and scattered things on the floor. A hooded officer with stars on
his shoulders appeared and ordered the two men holding me to force
me on my knees. He stood right in front of me. His black boots were
shining and he had a gun. His eyes glittered when he put the gun to
my head and cocked the trigger.

"Are you the owner?" he asked.

I didn't know how to answer and hesitated.

He pressed the gun to my forehead pushing my head back.

"Yes, I am the owner."

"Do you have a license from the ministry?"

"No," I said, "because—" but before I could finish telling him
that the place had been operating for decades without a license, he
slapped me with his gun and I fell down.

"Take him." They held me and started dragging me and I woke
up.

FORTY-EIGHT

I was at the *mghaysil* making the most of a respite without bodies and reading a book about Mesopotamian creation myths when I heard on the radio that a suicide bomber had attacked al-Mutanabbi Street and the Shahbandar café, killing more than thirty people. I felt a pang in my heart. We had gotten used to car and suicide bombs, but I had a soft spot for al-Mutanabbi Street. I would often escape there to hunt for a book or two to keep me company. I had bought the book I was reading from a stall there the Friday before.

I had decided not to work on Fridays. If my father were alive, he would have thought it blasphemous. I wondered whether the young man who sold me the book was hurt in the attack. I wondered naïvely, as I often did upon hearing such news: Why this spot in particular? Why go after books and booksellers who are barely making it?

In the evening, I saw the scenes of the aftermath that we have become accustomed to after each attack: puddles of blood, human remains, scattered shoes and slippers, smoke, and people standing in shock, wiping their tears or covering their faces. This time there were also remains of books and bloodstained paper waiting for someone to collect them and bury them. Professor al-Janabi called to tell me that one of my colleagues from the academy, Adil Mhaybis, had been killed in the attack. Adil wasn't a very close friend, but I knew him and we had chatted during our days at the academy. I'd seen him in recent years at the Hiwar gallery. He was very smart and ambitious and had started writing art reviews in newspapers. I asked whether Adil was married. Professor al-Janabi said that he was, and had left three kids. He promised to call me with funeral details.

I went to the funeral. Adil's father and brothers were sitting at the front of a tent pitched in front of the house. There was a huge picture of Adil, and a banner bore his name and the date of his martyrdom "during the cowardly terrorist attack on al-Mutanabbi Street." I shook hands with the father and brothers and offered my condolences, then sat in a corner and recited the *Fatiha* for his soul. I drank a cup of coffee with cardamom.

Al-Janabi was supposed to come, but he called and said that he was delayed by traffic and checkpoints. I looked around for a face I might know. Verses of the Qur'an were reverberating through the loudspeakers. The famous Egyptian reciter al-Minshawi had just finished the Joseph chapter in his mesmerizing voice and started the Rahman chapter, which my father had loved. The waves in his voice would touch one's soul gently at first and then pull it slowly until you found yourself suddenly at sea with nothing except the wind of the voice and the sails of the words. *"He created man from clay, like the potter"* caught my attention. So, we, too, are statues, but we never stop crushing one another in the name of the one who made us. We are statues whose permanent exhibition is dust.

"Which of the favors of your Lord will ye deny? Everyone on earth will perish . . . When the sky is rent asunder and becomes red."

Perhaps it *is* high time for him to crush what he has fashioned. I thought about this man who blew himself up and killed Adil and so many others. Who was he?

I try to find a rational explanation for such acts. I know that humans can reach a stage of anger and despair in which their lives have no value, and no other life or soul has value either. But men have been slaughtering others and killing themselves for ideas and symbols since time immemorial; what is new are the numbers of bodies becoming bombs. Al-Minshawi's arresting recitation began to weave through my thoughts.

"The guilty will be known by their marks and will be taken by their

forelocks and feet." Could that suicide bomber be there now, dragged by his hair and feet to a scorching fire?

"They go circling around between it and fierce, boiling water." "This is the Hell which the guilty deny." Will he be surprised by his fate and object to it, having thought that he was on his way to the two heavens? "Wherein is every kind of fruit in pairs." "Is there any reward for Good other than Good?"

And poor Adil, is he sitting in the shade under a palm tree or *"Reclining upon couches lined with silk brocade, the fruits of both gardens near to hand."* Will Adil see his killer dragged to hell and will he spit on him, or will he just look at him abhorrently? Will the two converse or argue in a neutral zone between heaven and hell? Or will they fight over getting into heaven?

"Which is it of the favors of your Lord that ye deny?"

Before getting a satisfying answer about Adil's fate, I saw one of the artists I had met at the exhibition at the French Cultural Center a few years before. I waved and he recognized me. He offered his condolences to Adil's family, then came and sat next to me. After reciting the *Fatiha*, we started chatting as we drank coffee. I was on my third cup. I asked whether Adil was a close friend of his. He said he was just an acquaintance, but he felt compelled to come. He looked weary and stressed out.

When I asked why, he said that he was leaving for Syria in two days because he had received death threats.

"Who is threatening you, and why?"

"Man. It's really absurd. I'm Shiite, but my son's name is Omar. I named him after my best friend, who happened to be Sunni. They left a note in front of the door threatening me and telling me to leave the neighborhood. They thought I was Sunni."

I asked him, "Who are 'they'?"

"I don't know really," he said. "Armed men who control the neighborhood and are killing left and right. I asked and looked around. I wanted someone to get the word to them that Abu Omar is not Sunni, but it was no use. Then I got another letter saying, 'This is the last warning. The next letter will not be written on paper and will pierce your head.' A week after that two bullets broke our bedroom window. Thank God, we weren't at home. They have forced a lot of Sunnis to leave. So we are living with my in-laws and we've decided to go to Syria until things calm down. Can you believe this? These four letters of a name. I just want to tell them, face to face, that I'm supposed to be one of their own. If they want me to change his name, I will, but just leave us alone."

When he finished his story, al-Minshawi was in the chapter of Abraham: "Lo, man is verily given up to injustice and ingratitude. And then Abraham said: Lord, make this city one of peace and preserve me and my sons from worshiping idols."

"I'm thinking of leaving too," I said. "Things are intolerable."

He nodded. "It's nice chatting with you, but I have a lot of errands to run and have to go."

We hugged outside the tent and I wished him luck in Syria.

FORTY-NINE

I saw you at the *mghaysil*, Father.

It was my first time at work with you. Hammoudy was not with us and it was pitch dark. You had a candle in your hand.

I asked you, "Why don't we wait until it's morning and then start work?"

You smiled and said, "There is nothing but night here."

I was surprised and asked, "Why?"

You said, "Have you forgotten that we are in the underworld, my son, and the sun doesn't rise here?"

I felt a lump in my throat and a tear found its way to my cheek.

You wiped it and hugged me saying in an unusually loving tone: "Don't worry, dear. Candles are enough for us to do our work and live a good life. You'll get used to their light."

It was the first time you ever called me "dear." You asked me to follow you and showed me the bench and said, "This is where we put together the body parts al-Fartusi brings every day." I was surprised that al-Fartusi was here as well.

You pointed to the cupboards, which I couldn't see clearly, and said, "The needles, threads and glue are all there." Then you pointed to wooden boxes which were stacked on the floor and said, "The feathers we use to cover the bodies are all in there."

I asked, "Why do we have to cover their bodies with feathers?"

You smiled and said, "Do you still ask too many questions, son? This is what our ancestors did before and what our grandchildren will keep doing."

You moved toward one of the cupboards and opened it. You took out a candle and lit it with the flame in your candle and handed it to me. I held it in my hand. Its flame illuminated more of the place. I saw legs and arms stacked in the corner and asked you about them.

"We will find a place for them in the bodies that come every day."

"What about Ammoury and Hammoudy and the others? Are they here too?"

You didn't answer. I saw an eye hanging on the wall by a thread and shedding tears. When I asked you about it you said, "It longs for another eye or perhaps it is crying for the sun."

I asked you: "Are we alive or dead, father?"

You didn't answer and blew out your candle and mine died too. I stayed alone in the dark listening to the tears falling from the eye on the wall until I woke up. The candle next to my head was choking and about to give out.

FIFTY

My mother put on her black abaya and said: "Jawad, I'm going to the shrine of al-Kazim. Today is the anniversary of his death, and Basim al-Karbala'i is coming to chant."

"Wait and we'll go together."

"Really?"

She was pleasantly surprised by my decision and her face lit up. She probably doesn't remember, just as I don't, the last time I visited the shrine. I used to go with her a lot when I was a child and would hold onto the window overlooking the tomb inside the shrine as the others did. Later I went often with my father, but I stopped in high school, when I became disenchanted with all the rituals and lost my faith.

She sat on the couch and said, "OK, I'll wait for you then."

I went up to my bedroom and changed. When I was coming down she asked me: "How come? Did you really remember al-Kazim, or is it just because al-Karbala'i is going to chant?"

"Can't it be both?"

"Yes, of course. A visit to al-Kazim is always a good thing."

I should have told her that I was seriously thinking of leaving the *mghaysil* for good and going to Jordan and then anywhere far away, but I never found the right words and time. I knew that I might not come back for a very long time, if ever. This might be the very last time I visited al-Kazim. I also wanted to listen to Basim al-Karbala'i's voice, which Mother herself had introduced me to by listening to him at home.

Kazimiyya's streets were teeming with pilgrims from all over the country. Security precautions were more severe than in previous years in anticipation of attacks, which had become common whenever large crowds of civilians gathered. A few mortar rockets had fallen in past years and car bombs had exploded more than once.

Hospitality stations offering water and food to pilgrims punctuated the streets, as did banners mourning the seventh imam and his death by poison in Haroun al-Rashid's prison. "Peace be upon the one who was tortured in dark prisons" and "O God pray for Muhammad and his family and pray for Musa the son of Ja'far, the guardian of the pious and the imam of the blessed. He of the long prostration and profuse tears." I saw a banner with the two famous lines by the poet al-Sharif al-Radi about the two shrines of Musa al-Kazim and Muhammad al-Jawad:

> *Two shrines in Baghdad heal my dejection and sorrow,*
> *Toward them I shall guide my soul and seek peace tomorrow.*

The two golden domes and four minarets glittered under the chains of lights, which linked them like tiny bridges. The light emanating from the shrine lit the sky. We parted at the iron fence and my mother went to the women's entrance. We agreed that I would meet her there an hour and a half later.

There was a long line to get in through the Murad gate on the eastern side. The armed national police were standing at the gate. The green neon lights at the top of the gate illuminated the engravings and verses adorning the arch of the door. Three men conducted a thorough search, making sure I hadn't hidden anything under my clothes or in my socks. I went inside and took off my shoes and handed them to an attendant.

I looked at the white marble walls and the ornaments and arabesques on the ceiling. I crossed through the golden gate to the courtyard of the mosque. There were hundreds of men and boys, all wearing black. Many crowded around the gates leading to the mausoleum. It looked impossible to gain entrance, and the crowd barely moved. I walked around in the courtyard thinking, *What would al-Kazim himself say to all these people were he alive today? Would he want them to come here and do what they were doing and say what they were saying?* Perhaps if he returned today he would be a stranger, just as he was in his time, perhaps even more of a stranger.

I looked at the two domes and minarets and then the black sky. My eyes descended again to the domes and then the entrance to the mausoleum. I started a silent conversation with al-Kazim. I told him: *Forgive me for not visiting you for so many years, but I have chosen another path. A path paved with doubt that doesn't lead to mosques. It is a rough and rugged path, not taken by crowds, with very few travel companions. I am still walking on it and I have ended up in prison just as you did, master. But I am imprisoned by my family and my people. I'm a prisoner of the death which has overtaken this land. It is time for me to escape. My mother is on the opposite side asking you to keep me by her side and by yours, but she might not realize that this daily death will poison me if I stay here.*

My silent conversation was interrupted by Basim al-Karbala'i's voice. He stood before the microphone to greet the hundreds of pilgrims who stood waiting for him. He took a piece of paper from his pocket and started to chant. His captivating voice struck deep in the heart:

> Where does this stranger come from?
> Where are his kith and kin?
> Of poison he died in prison
> No crime nor harm had he committed
> Woe unto the poisoned one!
> He spent his life grieving
> O Shiites when a man's wailing stops
> His loved ones surround him
> Some kiss and hug
> Others close his eyes.

Then he asked the crowd to chant along: "Where does this stranger come from? / Where are his kith and kin?" He urged us every now and then, saying, "Wail for your Imam and don't hold back."

Images and emotions crowded my inner domes: my heart and mind. All the statues I never sculpted and the drawings which remained sketches in my mind. Reem and her breast which was amputated, just as our love was. Ghayda' and her body which flew away like a dove. My father, Ammoury, and Hammoudy. The faces of the corpses I washed and shrouded on their way to the grave. Tears poured down and covered my face. I stayed in that open space, where I could cry without shame and without any explanation. My pain and wounds had a lung to breathe through. Forgive me Musa, son of Ja'far, for crying in your presence and on your day. I am a stranger among your visitors. I am a stranger like you and I am crying for myself.

FIFTY-ONE

"Alas," al-Fartusi said with genuine sadness when I informed him that I was going to Jordan.

"Why? Why are you going and leaving us?"

"I can't do it anymore. I'm suffocating. I'm not cut out for this job. I wasn't planning on doing it for two years. I can't sleep at night. Nightmares are driving me insane."

He patted me on the shoulder and said: "You think I'm any better? I've gotten diabetes and high blood pressure from everything I've seen all these years. And now these crooks want to fabricate charges against me."

"What charges?"

"They want to implicate me in selling human organs. Can you believe that? There are gangs selling human organs. They have entire networks and there were stories about it in newspapers, but that's all linked to the hospitals. We have nothing to do with that, because organs have to be harvested from the body within a few hours."

"Why are they accusing you, then?"

"Someone somewhere wants to make some money, and they just want a bribe to stop harassing me."

"I'm sorry. You of all people don't deserve this. I hope it works out."

"Whatever God wills will happen. This is my destiny and if you are destined to leave, then you will leave. I wish you the very best. But why don't you pray? I bet you these nightmares will go away."

"God has yet to guide me to the right path. Plus, my nightmares are really something else."

He shook his head and laughed. I gave him the keys to the *mghaysil* and we agreed that he would send me the rent in Amman. As we hugged and kissed goodbye, I asked him to take care of Mahdi.

"I'll treat him like a son," he said.

FIFTY-TWO

The earth was a carpet of sleeping sand stretching from horizon to horizon, nothing disrupting it except the highway on which cars escaped from hell to the unknown. We were part of a convoy of four GMC station wagons. We started out early in the morning so as to avoid the desert darkness that might make us easy prey for the thieves and to make sure we reached the Jordanian border before sunset.

Abu Hadi, our driver, was in his late thirties. He had short black hair and a neatly trimmed moustache. He was overdressed and wore his sunglasses even before the sun was strong. Like all other drivers he had a gun that he hid under the seat before we left. I sat next to him. The other passengers were a man in his fifties and his wife and three daughters. The eldest was seventeen, the youngest about eight or nine. They were all veiled. The girls spent most of the trip asleep. The father exchanged short conversations with his wife about the food they had brought along. The father had hesitated at first when he saw that I, a strange man, was coming along, but Abu Hadi lied, saying that I was his cousin, and that calmed him.

Abu Hadi was silent most of the trip. I was left with my thoughts and worries as I reviewed my options in Amman and the potential consequences of this trip. Every now and again Abu Hadi uttered a few short sentences telling us how many hours of travel remained.

I knew that obtaining permanent residency in Amman was almost impossible. According to the latest restriction, only those who could deposit a hundred thousand dollars in a Jordanian bank were awarded residency. I didn't have even one tenth of that. As for getting a visa or asylum elsewhere, that too was quite difficult. Professor al-Janabi had promised in his last e-mail to help me get settled in the first few weeks. I had his address and phone number.

It was too dangerous to carry a lot of cash, so I arranged with my sister to transfer what I had saved in the last two years to a bank in Jordan once I got settled there. Getting into Jordan wasn't always guaranteed.

I felt a bit hungry and reached into the small bag I'd put between my feet and opened the plastic bag inside it. My mother had insisted on making me the walnut-and-date-filled klaycha I liked, filling a whole bag with them. I had brought along a few other things and the book on Mesopotamian creation myths. I had packed one big suitcase. It was tough to decide what to take and what to leave behind. I took plenty of winter clothes, because I had heard that Amman's winter was severe. I also took two photo albums, which contained many of my photographs from my academy years, as well as of my own works and sketches. And I packed some of my note-books.

The night before, when I came down the stairs carrying the suitcase to put it next to the door, my mother asked whether I needed help. She leaned on the wall and put her right hand on her cheek and said: "I still can't believe that you're leaving." She started to cry.

I hugged her. "You can come visit me in Amman or wherever I end up. I will visit."

"I don't believe you. You'll never come back."

She had tried to dissuade me from leaving for the last few days, but I had made up my mind and told her that I couldn't go on as I had been, that I was suffocating and dying. I left the suitcase by the door to pick it up the next morning before leaving. I gave my mother enough money for a year, and we went to my sister's new house in Karrada. I wasn't going to let my mother stay alone at her age and in these circumstances.

In that taxi ride that my mother and I took from our house to my sister's, I felt for the hundredth time what a stranger I'd become in my hometown and how my alienation had intensified in these last years. I recalled a line of verse I liked: "One is not a stranger in Syria or Yemen, but is truly a stranger in his shroud and grave." But the stranger today was whoever lived in Rusafah and Karkh, Baghdad's two halves. Everyone in Baghdad felt like a stranger in his own country. Most people were drained, and the fatigue was clearly drawn on their faces.

I wondered how they went on despite everything. How did they manage to wake up every morning and try? But was there any other choice? Was I just too weak? Thousands of others were running away from this civil war whose end no one can predict.

When would this war tire of slaughtering people and just quit? Not just stop to catch its breath before continuing to tear away at the country, but really quit. I always used to say that Baghdad in Saddam's time was a prison of mythic dimensions. Now the prison had fragmented into many cells with sectarian dimensions, separated by high concrete walls and bloodied by barbed wires.

We were approaching al-Firdaws Square, where Saddam's gigantic statue used to stand. I remembered how I saw them years earlier taking down the old monument of the Unknown Soldier, which used to occupy this square and was much more beautiful than the new Unknown Soldier monument. Now, propelled by the illusion of erasing the past and forcibly disfiguring the present, the new Saddams were taking down statues left and right. As if there was a giant axe snatched by each new regime from its predecessor to continue the destruction and deepen the grave. *What good are all these metaphors*, I wondered.

My sister and her husband, Sattar, had moved to a new house he'd bought in Karrada. It was the fruit of his agility in riding the new wave, just as he had ridden the previous one under Saddam. Her husband was a "comrade" in the past, and he had kept defending the *ancien régime* and its policies vigorously even in its last few years. Sattar and my father once had a terrible argument. Sattar left our house and swore never to set foot in it again. He only did so after my father's death. Although he had forced my sister to stay away from the family, she would still visit from time to time. My father's death finally patched things up. I'd never liked Sattar and had had doubts about him during their engagement, but she loved him and he treated her well.

We got lost in al-Karrada's streets with its big houses. I called my sister on the cell phone to get directions, repeating everything she said to the taxi driver. She said she was going to stand outside to wave when she saw us. I spotted her in a side street ten minutes later and told the driver to back up to that street. I asked him to wait for me while I said goodbye, but my mother objected: "Why are you in such a hurry?" My sister also chastised me for not having visited her new house or seen her kids in months. I hesitated and looked at the garage. Her husband's car was not there. As if sensing what I was thinking, she reassured me, "Come on. Come on in. Let's get enough of you before you leave. Sattar isn't home and won't be back until later tonight, and the kids are in school." I paid the taxi driver and we all went in.

Their house had a big garden. The lawn was neatly trimmed and framed by flowers on all sides. I spotted some carnations. The palm tree's fronds in the far right corner were touching a window on the second floor. Its bunches were full of dates. A white metal table, surrounded by four chairs, sat on the white and yellow marble of the walkway in front of the house. We went in through the kitchen door. My sister had put plenty of flowerpots by the window and filled them with the cactus plants she loved. The house had been recently built. It had five bedrooms, three bathrooms, and a huge living room. My sister had prepared one of the bedrooms on the ground floor close to the bathroom for my mother to sleep in. That way she wouldn't have to strain her knees going up and down the stairs.

"Look how beautiful your room is," my sister said proudly, and I felt she was addressing me as well. My mother kissed her on the cheek and thanked her. I put Mom's suitcase next to her new bed. The room had a medium-sized cupboard and a huge mirror and two red chairs, one in front of the mirror and the other next to a TV table. Above the TV, the room's only window overlooked the neighbor's garden.

"I'm making okra stew. I know you love it. Why don't you stay?" my sister said. "It'll be ready in an hour."

"I have a few appointments and have to be somewhere. I'll have tea."

"Tea it shall be."

She took us to the living room and I sat down. The TV was turned to one of the local satellite channels and was showing the gory aftermath of a suicide bombing in al-Karkh that had taken place half an hour before. We had left Mother in her room unpacking. Minutes later she came and sat next to me and said she would finish settling in later. "I want to get enough of you."

My sister came back with a tray full of cookies and some plates and forks, putting it on the big table in the middle. She pulled a smaller table from under it and put it in front of me. She put two cookies on a plate and put it on the table in front of me. She looked at the TV screen and said, "Ah, when will these suicide bombers leave us alone? Haven't they had enough?" Mom invoked God and put her hand on her cheek.

The images of scattered body parts and pools of blood reminded me of what I was escaping, but I couldn't avoid thinking of the fate of these corpses. Who would wash them and shroud them? I asked my sister to change the channel. She handed me the remote and went to the kitchen to check on the tea. I kept turning the channels until I found one showing a nature documentary with birds. I bit into one of the cookies.

The TV was on the middle shelf of a huge entertainment center made of Indian oak. On some of the shelves were china and crystal. Another bore some books, but I couldn't see their titles. The shelf right above the TV had framed pictures of my nephew and niece, Maysam and Muthanna, a family photo, and then a photo of the head of the household, wearing a suit and a tie, shaking hands and smiling with one of the ministers. I remembered their old house, with a much smaller TV, and on top a framed photo of Sattar and some of his comrades with Saddam. Saddam had rewarded him for his loyalty during his years of service to the Ba'th Party. I wondered what Sattar had done with that photo. Had it been fed to the fire, or was it hiding in a box somewhere in case a new strategic change might be needed in the future?

My sister brought in the teapot. I was about to ask her about this new loyalty, but why say goodbye with an argument? It was strange that the de-Ba'thification Law didn't apply to Sattar, even though it had affected so many others. My sister poured the tea and put one spoon of sugar in the cup for me. I could smell the cardamom.

My mother asked her about Sattar and his health.

She answered that he was well, but always busy and coming home late. He was traveling to Turkey for work and she and the kids had been sleeping at his family's house for safety, but the new house was in a very safe area.

My sister asked me about the *mghaysil* and what I'd decided to do with it.

I told her I had agreed to lease it to al-Fartusi, who would hire someone to work there.

Mom put down her cup and started to wipe away tears. She repeated what had become a mantra in these recent weeks: "But where will you go, son?"

When she started sobbing, I decided that it was time to leave. My heart almost stopped when she held on to me as if she knew it would be the last time she would see me.

"You all went away and left me. I'm gonna die before I see you again," she said, her words soaked in tears.

My sister was offended: "What's this, Mom? Don't I count? God forgive you." My sister hugged and kissed me. She shed a few tears, but reassured me, saying, "Don't worry about her at all."

My mother insisted on sprinkling water as I was leaving, a charm supposed to guarantee my return. She kept repeating, "Call us when you get there." I waved to them both and had a feeling that maybe she was right: I might not see her again for a long time, maybe ever.

I couldn't identify the feelings that overtook me after I left. After the sadness I felt as I was saying goodbye to them, I was overtaken by guilt toward my mother, but I also thought of the dead. Who would wash them now?

When we arrived at the Traybeel Center on the Iraqi side of the border, we joined a long line of parked cars. Many passengers had gotten out and sat or squatted nearby. As our convoy took its place, the driver said that the line was normal; it might take a few hours, especially since there had been explosions in Jordan recently. He got out of the car and went to chat with other drivers who had gathered. I got out to stretch. The last time we'd stopped was five hours before. The man in the back seat got out and started walking on the shoulder of the road, holding his worry beads. His beads had kept ticking throughout the trip, reminding me of my father.

I noticed that every now and then a few cars headed back in the opposite direction, toward Baghdad. After about half an hour the line started to move. Our driver got in and inched forward. He motioned to me to get in, but I told him that I was going to walk. The line stopped after a few minutes. I told the driver that I was going to keep walking ahead. He took a drag on his cigarette and said, "Sure, just don't get lost."

"How can I? It's all desert!" I said.

I walked for fifteen minutes. A man asked me for a light for his cigarette. I apologized, saying that I didn't smoke.

He laughed and seemed astonished, as if I were the only non-smoker in the world. "How can you bear living without smoking?"

"I don't know," I shrugged. Then: "How I can bear living?"

He smiled and asked, "Leaving alone?"

"Yes."

"They're saying that single men aren't allowed in. Only families."

"Why?"

"I dunno, man. They're saying they're afraid of Shiite militias. I mean, we're running away from the militias and terrorism."

I had included not being allowed into Jordan on my list of contingencies, but I had allowed myself to imagine my escape from the hell I was shackled with. The man's words reminded me that my plan might fail.

I went back and got into the car. It took us two hours to get through. Before we arrived at the al-Ruwayshid border point on the Jordanian side, dozens of tents with ropes and clothes hanging between them appeared on the side of the road. The United Nations' blue flag flew over the camp. The driver noticed me turning back to look. "It's a camp for the Palestinians who were kicked out of their homes in Baladiyyat," he said. "A lot of them were killed. They've been here for more than a couple of years now."

The woman in the back seat chimed in: "They flourished under Saddam and now they'll get a taste of the torture we got for so many years."

Her comment brought her husband back from his snooze, and he scolded her. "God Almighty. They didn't get any more than many others did. Poor people. Have some mercy in your heart, woman."

"I don't have a heart anymore," she answered.

I thought of what she said. Most hearts were so fatigued, they ran away from their bodies, leaving behind caves in which beasts sleep.

After we waited an hour at al-Ruwayshid, the Jordanian officer eyeballed me with tired eyes and asked me rather coarsely: "Anyone with you?"

"No, just me."

He threw aside my passport, saying:

"No single men. Only families get in."

"But why?"

"These are the orders." He motioned for me to leave and yelled "Next!"

Abu Hadi, the driver, brought down my suitcase from the trunk and gave me back half of the fee. He patted me on the shoulder saying, "Try to go to Syria. It's much easier. Or just wait until things calm down a bit and give it another try." We said goodbye and the man who was waiting with his family in the car waved to me. I waved back. Abu Hadi drove away. I tried to send a text message to al-Janabi, but there was no network. I would have to write to my uncle.

The number of those who weren't allowed into Jordan was enough to start a service from the border back to Baghdad's stabbed heart. I saw a driver yelling from the window of his car "One passenger to Baghdad. One to Baghdad." I walked over carrying my suitcase, heavy with disappointment. I would have to write to both my uncle and al-Janabi about this. Would Ghayda' believe me?

FIFTY-THREE

One of the old Mesopotamian creation myths says that for a long time the gods used to do their work and fulfill their tasks. Some planted, some harvested, and others made things. But they were tired, so they complained to An-ki, the god of water and wisdom, and asked him to lighten their burden. But he was in the depths of the water and did not hear their complaints. So the gods resorted to his mother, Nammu.

She went and called out to him, "Rise up, son, and create slaves for the gods."

An-ki thought about it, then summoned the crafts gods to make humans out of clay. He told his mother: "The creatures I have decided to make will be in the image of the gods. Scoop some mud from the deep waters and give it to the crafts gods to knead and thicken into clay, then you make the body parts with the help of Mother Earth."

Thus humans were created to carry the burden of the gods and their toil. An-ki said to the great gods, "I will prepare a pure place and one of the gods shall be slaughtered there. Let the other gods be baptized with his blood. We will mix his flesh and blood with the clay and he shall be both god and human, eternally united in clay."

FIFTY-FOUR

We finished washing and shrouding a nine-year-old boy. He needed only wings to look like an angel. He was killed with his father in an explosion next to the National Theater. I felt my ribs stabbing me from within and strangling my every breath. I told Mahdi that I was going outside to sit next to the pomegranate tree. I'd been sitting the last few months on the chair I'd put in front of it to converse with it. It has become my only companion in the world. Its red blossoms had opened like wounds on the branches, breathing and calling out. I'd been humming a song I heard a few weeks before and replaced "Sweet Basil" with "Pomegranate" in its lyrics.

Pity me, pity me
O Pomegranate tree
I've become skin and bones
And nobody knows
My malady
And nobody knows
My remedy
Pity me, pity me
O Pomegranate tree

I looked at its dark soil, wet with the washing water it had just drunk. *It's a wondrous tree*, I thought. Drinking the water of death for decades now, but always budding, blossoming, and bearing fruit every spring. Is that why my father loved it so much? He used to tell me that the Prophet Muhammad said there is a seed from paradise in every pomegranate fruit. But paradise is always somewhere else.

And hell, all of it, is here and grows bigger every day. Like me, this pomegranate's roots were here in the depths of hell.

Do the roots reveal everything to the branches, or do they keep what is painful to themselves? Its branches rise up and when the wind toys with them, they look like they are fluttering and about to fly. But it's a tree. Its fate is to be a tree and to remain here. I keep saying that I don't believe in fate. So why am I saying this? I should say its history, not its fate. History is what people call fate. And history is random and violent, storming and uprooting everything and everyone without ever turning back.

A beautiful nightingale perched on one of the pomegranate's high branches. The nightingale turned its black head and gazed at me with its black eyes. Its head was adorned with a white triangular crown. It turned its head again and I saw its cheek was the same white as its tail feathers.

It started singing with a gentle sweetness—as if it knew I had complained that paradise was far away, so it had brought its sound right here. Are you thinking of building a nest here? Does my presence worry you? Don't be afraid. I'm not an enemy. I remembered the nightingale we had in a cage at home when I was a child. My father used to feed it pieces of dates, apples, grapes, and pomegranate.

The living die or depart, and the dead always come. I had thought that life and death were two separate worlds with clearly marked boundaries. But now I know they are conjoined, sculpting each other. My father knew that, and the pomegranate tree knows it as well.

Mahdi opened the door and said: "Jawad, they brought one."

The nightingale fled. I sighed and said, "Okay, I'm coming. Just give me another minute."

I am like the pomegranate tree, but all my branches have been cut, broken, and buried with the dead. My heart has become a shriveled pomegranate beating with death and falling every second into a bottomless pit.

But no one knows. No one. The pomegranate alone knows.

ACKNOWLEDGMENTS

John Donatich for his elegant edits and suggestions.

Richard Sieburth, my cornerman, for his friendship and support, and for carefully and gracefully editing the text.

Ibtisam Azem, my love, my *first* and best reader, for her critical suggestions, advice, and support. And for being in my life.